"A good hockey player plays where the puck is. A great hockey player plays where the puck is going to be."

—Wayne Gretzky

OTHER BOOKS BY SAM & BEN

Hockey Wars Series

Hockey Wars

Hockey Wars 2 - The New Girl

Hockey Wars 3 - The Tournament

Hockey Wars 4 - Championships

Hockey Wars 5 - Lacrosse Wars (Coming Spring 2020)

My Little Series

The Day My Fart Followed Me Home

The Day My Fart Followed Me To Hockey

The Day My Fart Followed Santa Up The Chimney

The Day My Fart Followed Me To Soccer

The Day My Fart Followed Me To The Dentist

The Day My Fart Followed Me To The Zoo

The Day My Fart Followed Me To Baseball

It's Not Easy Being A Little Fart

If I Was A Caterpillar

1

MILLIE AND THE other girls from her team were sitting around with Cameron and a few of the other boys from the boys team, stretching and chatting while both teams waited for their field lacrosse game to start. It was almost the end of the field lacrosse season, and both the boys' and girls' teams were playing on the same field for once.

Usually, they played on opposite sides of town, on different days and at different times. It was nice to be able to hang out together between games and relax. Some of the parents had brought a BBQ and food, and a tailgate party had popped up in the carpark.

Soon summer would be over, and the long hot days would be gone, but it wasn't all bad news. The end of summer meant the start of something else: hockey! Lacrosse was fun, but hockey was everyone's favorite sport, and both the boys and girls were hoping to have an amazing season this year. The girls had a real shot at taking the championship.

As the girls waited for their game to start, they talked about who they were playing in their last lacrosse game of the regular season coming up next weekend. The Baxter Panthers. Bleh. They all knew they didn't have a chance. The Panthers had smashed them earlier in the season, and the next game would probably be much the same.

Unfortunately, they weren't going to make it into the field lacrosse finals this year. Neither team had managed to put together a great season in the win department, but they'd all had a blast playing and hoped that next year they would come out a lot stronger.

"OMG! You won't believe what I heard my mom talking about with your mom, V!" Daylyn blurted out as she came running up to where the two teams were laying around.

Concern and confusion flashed across Violet's face as she waited for Daylyn to finish speaking.

"Well, what is it, Daylyn?"

"Apparently, the coaches are making some big

announcement at tonight's preseason meeting," blurted out Daylyn, not able to hold it in any longer.

"Aaand...what's this big announcement?" Millie asked impatiently. Just once it would be nice if Daylyn could get to the point without turning everything into a total drama.

"Day, come on. We already knew that. They sent all of our parents that email. Remember?" Georgia said, just a little bit confused about the whole thing.

"What I think they're all asking you, Day, is what did you hear exactly? What's the big news?" laughed Cameron. *Girls*, Cameron thought, *everything has to be a big production.* "Get to the point already!"

"If you would all stop talking for just one minute, I would tell you!" huffed Daylyn, crossing her arms and pouting. "As I was trying to say before all of you so rudely interrupted me, I totally overheard my mom say that the coaches are introducing a new girl to our team tonight!" Daylyn said, trying to get it all out before someone else interrupted.

"OMG!" they all said in unison. This wasn't good news. Chaos erupted as all the girls tried to speak over each other.

"We already have a full team?"

"Where is the new girl going to play?"

"What position will she play?"

"Will one of us lose our spot?"

"We already had tryouts. I'm not losing my spot!"

Cameron stood up and looked around at the other boys, motioning them to follow him. "WOW," he mouthed silently, looking around as the other boys followed his lead and stood up as well, moving away from the girls who were now all huddled together.

"Umm, that was totally intense," Hunter said as the boys looked over at the girls who were now wildly waving their hands around.

"You're telling me, buddy," Cameron replied.

"I wonder if she's cute?" Luke asked.

"You wish!" Logan said, ducking away as Luke tried to grab him in a headlock.

A siren sounded, announcing the end of the games currently underway out on the field.

"All right guys, we have to go out and warm up. Get your gear and meet me down at the far end of the field. Luke, you start them stretching, and I'll be there in a minute," Cameron said as he picked up his lacrosse stick and started walking towards where Millie sat with the other girls, who were all still losing their minds . The boys nodded and started jogging down to the far end of the field.

"Mills?" Cameron called out as he walked towards her. "Mills!"

"What!? I mean, umm, what, Cam?" Millie asked, still trying to hear what the other girls were talking about.

"The siren just went."

"So, what? Oh, crap! Right! Thanks! I owe you!"

"No worries," Cameron said, laughing as he walked away shaking his head. Girls. Just when you think you've got them all figured out you learn something new. Who would have thought that getting a new player would cause so much chaos? At least his team wasn't getting any new players this season.

"Okay, girls! Grab your gear and get out on the field. We only have a few minutes to warm up!" Millie shouted, panicking, as she looked around for her lacrosse stick.

"I wonder if the new girl plays center?" Khloe shouted as she struggled to put her goalie pads on, watching a horrified expression come over Millie's face.

"I heard she was a goalie!" Violet shouted back with a big grin on her face.

"Shut up! There is no way!" Khloe looked horrified.

"Enough! We have a game to play. Let's worry about the new girl after we finish this game. Let's go, team, long lap. Let's go!" Millie shouted, leading her team on a run around the outside of the field.

It was easy enough to say it, Millie thought, but what if the new girl did play center, and what if she was good? Millie knew that she was good—that's why she was the captain—but there was always a little doubt that someone could come along and steal her spot away from her. Enough! Millie thought to herself as the team ran around the field. Focus on today's game; worry about the rest later.

2

"HURRY UP, MILLIE, or we're going to be late!" Millie's mother yelled from the top of the stairs.

Bang, bang, thump, bang.

"Millie Anne! I've told you before! Be careful with your bag, and don't you dare scratch up those walls."

"Sorry, mom. I swear, every season this bag just seems to get heavier and heavier." Millie huffed and puffed as she finally threw her large hockey bag down at the top of the stairs. The bag felt like it was full of rocks.

"Have you got your socks?"

"Umm, yeah, I'm pretty sure I have everything."

"You're pretty sure, huh? That's good because I'm not driving back from the arena again because you only have one skate."

"That was one time mom. One time!"

"One time was one time too many. I have a good idea. Maybe you could try cleaning out your hockey bag for a change! You're ten years old now Millie, plenty old enough to start taking care of your own hockey equipment."

"I know, I know, mom. I'll do it tonight after practice. I promise!"

"Yeah, I've heard that promise before, miss. Your bag stinks, FYI. A little bit longer and it'll grow legs and be able to carry itself around the house. I feel bad for all your poor friends who have to sit with you in the change room. They must love it," Millie's mom said, laughing and holding her nose, fanning the air around her.

"Mom, all our bags stink. Stop being so dramatic. That's hockey!" Millie said with a laugh, dragging her bag out of the house and pushing the door shut behind her.

The drive to the arena was quiet. Unusually quiet. Millie was thinking about the new girl and trying to think of ways she could slip it into the non-existent conversation. They were pulling into the carpark by the time Millie finally decided to just blurt it out.

"Hey, mom. Umm, do you know anything about the new girl that's supposed to be joining my team?" Millie asked as they drove towards the door. *If the parents got an email from the coach, then mom should know something*, Millie thought to herself. You'd think they'd tell the captain before the rest of the team.

"Well, Coach Phil really wanted to announce it to the whole team at once. In the email, he asked us not to say anything, so I guess you'll have to wait and see."

"Mom! I'm the captain. Surely I can know *something* before the rest of the team." Millie said with a huff, crossing her arms. Millie's mom laughed.

"Millie, I love you, but if Coach Phil wants to tell you as a group, then that's what's going to happen," Millie's mom said, pulling the brake on and switching off the car's ignition. "Look, Millie, I know you have your team, and you're all best friends, but things change, okay?" Millie nodded slowly, looking out the window.

Millie couldn't help but feel nervous about the whole thing. So many questions were running through her head, she just couldn't switch them off. *Will this hurt the team? We're such a close group, and I don't want anything to hurt that. What if she plays my position? What if she wants to be captain? Will I lose my friends? Ahh. Stop, brain.*

"I know, mom."

"Sometimes things change, and it can seem like everything sucks at the time, but then it turns out for the best. Just do me a favor. Give this new girl a fair chance. No one likes being the 'new girl,' so make her feel welcome. You're the captain, and it's up to you to lead by example for the rest of your team. Now, get your stinking hockey gear out of my trunk and get your butt moving, miss!"

"Okay, mom. Thanks."

"Anytime. Now, get a move on captain, or you'll be late!"

Millie walked into the large meeting room and threw her hockey bag and stick down with all the other girl's bags. Great, she was the last one to arrive. *Some captain*, she thought to herself.

"Have you seen her?" Khloe asked Millie as she joined the huddle of girls.

"No, where is she?" Millie asked, craning her

neck trying to look around the room, all the while trying not to be too obvious.

"Just over there with her mom. You can't really see her from here."

"Attention, everyone. Okay everyone, listen up!" shouted Coach Phil. "I want everyone to welcome Mia to the Dakota Hurricanes. Okay, now Mia is a late transfer, but if we want to win this year, we can always use the help. Besides, Kate's dad had to transfer last minute for work, so we were a player short. Stand up and say hi, Mia."

Mia stood up slowly and looked around the large room. "Hi." Mia could feel her face go red. *OMG, how embarrassing*, she thought, dropping back into her seat. The other girls in the room whispered back and forth amongst each other.

"Okay girls, shush now. Moving onto other items..." Coach Phil went on for about another twenty minutes, talking about the upcoming schedule, tournaments, and what he expected from parents and players. *It was the same speech he gave every year before the start of the season*, Millie thought to herself, sneaking glances over at the new girl.

"Right. That's it from me. Girls, head out and hit the change room. I'll see you on the ice in twenty minutes."

As the girls sat down in their usual spots in the change room, Millie couldn't help but notice how quiet it was. Usually, they would be mucking around, talking and laughing. Now, it was oddly quiet. She didn't want to, but someone had to introduce the team, and she was the captain after all.

Brrraaapp.

"OMG, Khloe!" Violet yelled. "Did you just fart?"

Khloe looked around the change room as she stood up. "Yup!" she said with a wink to the new girl, before walking out. Well, that was it. The whole room burst into laughter. Millie couldn't help herself, joining in with the rest of the team. *What was wrong with goalies?* Millie thought to herself. *They're such a bunch of weirdos.*

The tension in the change room was gone, and now all the girls were chatting and laughing as usual. Millie finally pulled herself together and stood up to introduce herself to Mia.

"Hi, I'm Millie. I'm the captain. That weird goalie that just walked out is Khloe. You'll love her. The other senior girls are Georgia, who plays right wing, Lola on the left wing, Ashlyn on defense, Daylyn another D, and Sage and Violet, our forwards. I play center. The juniors are Emma, Isabelle, Aniyah, Maizie, Kiera, and Maddie. What position do you play?

"Nice to meet you all. Umm, I always played center on my old team." Mia replied standing up and looking around the room. Millie felt her stomach drop. Of course, she played center. *It was going to be a long day*, Millie thought to herself as she walked out of the change room.

3

AS THE GIRLS skated out on to the ice, something just didn't feel right. It was as if the team's dynamics were off. When a team played together for years, they started to learn when something wasn't working, and the new girl, Mia, was making everything seem just a little bit weird and awkward.

Khloe was warming up in front of the goalie net, stretching and sliding from side to side to warm her muscles up. A lot of people think goalies have it easy in the net, but the truth is it takes a special kind of person to remain ready and focused for an entire game. You never knew when that shot was going to come screaming in.

Khloe couldn't help but notice how the team had separated itself from Mia. Not a lot, but enough that Mia was definitely feeling it. She was doing her own warm-up routine, and from where Khloe was watching, she looked like she was good.

Damn, she's good, really good. Millie thought to herself as she started her own warm up.

"All right, ladies, front and center!" Coach Phil shouted as he skated out to the center of the arena. "Millie, I want you to put them through their paces. Get them lined up for the weaving drill, run it through first, and the rest of you line up behind Millie on the line. Khloe?"

"Yes, coach?" Khloe spun around. She hadn't been paying attention. She was watching Mia. The new girl was very pretty, she thought to herself, and those skates looked amazing.

"Are you ready, or would you like us all to take a five-minute break while you stare off into space?" The girls all giggled to themselves, but a quick glare from the coach soon wiped the smirks off their faces.

"Yes, coach. Ready, coach." Khloe replied with an awkward curtsy in her pads and a wink to the other girls. Coach Phil rolled his eyes and looked down at his skates. It was going to be one of *those* practices.

Millie was front and center on the line. *Why*

was she so nervous? Millie asked herself. Why couldn't she get it together today? Mia was standing directly behind her in the line, and Millie knew she was probably watching her. She couldn't afford to muck this up if she wanted to be the starting center.

Millie dodged between each cone quickly and made it all the way through quickly without once losing the puck. A quick slide to her preferred shooting side and a flick of the wrist saw the puck slide into the goal.

"Damn, Mills, you know that's my worst side. Unfair!" Khloe shouted, lying on her side in the crease.

"Tough break, Go Low!" Millie said with a laugh. Khloe growled. They'd been calling Khloe Go Low since she saved a goal by sliding on her face and letting the puck bounce off her helmet's visor.

"Great job, Millie! Nice stick handling and better luck next time, Khloe. Next!" Coach Phil shouted. Maybe there was some hope for this practice after all.

Now it was Mia's turn. She couldn't afford to make a mess of this. It was never easy being the new girl, and she knew from experience everyone would be watching to see how good she was.

Mia planted her skate and was off, rolling the puck along the blade of her stick as she ducked and weaved through the small orange cones. As she skated past the last cone, Mia faked to the left and then flicked to the right.

Khloe scrambled to recover from the fake out, but she wasn't going to get back in time. The puck arched up over Khloe's leg as she stretched for all she was worth. *Nope, wasn't going to happen*, she thought as the puck slipped into the back of the net.

"Nice shot!" Georgia said as Mia skated past her. Millie threw her head around and looked at Georgia with a puzzled expression. "What? She's good." Georgia was Millie's best friend, and she knew it would drive her crazy, but she liked to stir things up every now and again. Millie was a great skater and center, but she could get a big head about being captain sometimes.

"Great job, Mia! Khloe, I want you to try and read their bodies more. They'll show you what direction they'll go. Next up!" Coach Phil shouted. Georgia started her run down the cones, but Millie was still staring at Mia.

Millie shook herself and came back to reality. *Focus girl!* she thought to herself as she closed her mouth. *It's time to start worrying.* Millie could hear a few of the junior girls talking to Mia at the back of the line and asking her how she got so good at skating and shooting.

The rest of the practice went much like the first drill. Millie was trying to be on the top of her game, and so was Mia. Both players had a wicked competitive streak, and neither was willing to give up any advantage. The rest of the team hadn't failed to miss the growing tension between their captain and Mia. You would have to be blind as a bat to miss it.

Millie skated off the ice as soon as the coach yelled for them to hit the change rooms. She usually hung around until the end, but all the girls were talking to Mia, and she couldn't deal with it right now. She'd never been like this with anyone before, and she didn't like the way it was making her feel and act.

"Right, before we all start getting changed, let me just say great first practice. With a little focus and hard work, I think you all have a great chance of finishing on top of the division this year. Don't let it go to your head, though. There's still a long way to go in the season. It's still going to take some hard work. Okay, enough from me. I'll see you all at the next practice," Coach Phil said to the girls.

Millie changed with lightning speed and walked through the arena to the carpark. She needed to get out of here and try and get her thoughts together.

"Great job, Millie," her mom said to her as she slipped into the passenger seat.

"Yeah, thanks," Millie replied looking out the window. Yep. *It was going to be a long season*, she thought to herself.

4

THE FINAL LACROSSE game went about as well as both the boys' and the girls' teams had expected it to. They lost. They weren't destroyed, but neither team really stood a chance. That's not to say they didn't have a blast playing field lacrosse, and they would definitely be back and be even more competitive next year.

"So, my parents said it was cool if everyone wanted to come over for a swim and BBQ today," Preston said, throwing his lacrosse bag over his shoulder. Preston's parents were super rich. They owned their own plane-leasing company. Rich and famous people could lease or rent planes from them or charter them for trips and stuff. Preston never bragged about it, but he had heaps of posters and headshots of famous people in his bedroom.

A quick round of cools, yeps, and sweets went around the group of boys and girls sitting on the grass.

"Okay, so anytime around lunch is good. Bring your swimmers and towels. Dad has all the BBQ food ready, so he told me to tell you to tell your parents they didn't need to bring anything. See ya's later!" Preston said with a smile and a wave as he walked away towards the carpark.

"You going, Mills?" Cameron asked Millie.

"Umm, yeah, are you?" *Well, it was a warm day*, Millie thought to herself, *so why not*. There wasn't going to be many more of them. In a few months, the cold would well and truly set in.

"Of course. I love the BBQs at Preston's. His mom makes that awesome Mexican corn. I don't know what the secret is or how she makes it, but it tastes so good!"

"Mayonnaise and parmesan cheese, doofus. My mom makes it for me too!" Millie said with a laugh. It was one of her favorites too. Another thing her and Cameron had in common.

"Anyway, my dad's waiting for me, so I better get going. I'll see you at Preston's!"

"Okay. See you there," Millie replied, watching Cameron say goodbye to his team as he walked towards the carpark. *He really was dreamy*, she thought. *Jeez, Millie, get a grip. He's your best friend and you only just made up.*

"Millie! Let's go. I have a client calling in thirty minutes!" Millie's mom shouted from the carpark.

"Okay, mom! I'm coming. Jeez." Millie said as she got up and jogged to the carpark.

The day had turned out even better than expected. It was as if summer was having one last going-away party. Millie was floating around in the pool on a blow-up mattress, talking with Georgia and Lola about the last game of field lacrosse and how they thought they would do in hockey this season.

"OMG, Mills, Khloe bought Mia," Lola said as all three girls looked up at the two new arrivals.

"Hey Mills, who's the new girl?" Rhys asked from the other side of the pool.

"That's Mia, goofball. She just joined our team," Georgia said splashing water across to where Rhys was leaning against the side of the pool watching Khloe and Mia walk in.

"Can she skate?" Hunter asked.

"Please. She can skate circles around the lot of you!" Lola said with a laugh.

"We've only had one practice. Let's wait and see before we declare her the best of the best, shall we?" Millie said quietly.

"Woah. Someone sounds like they're a bit threatened, huh Mills?" Rhys said with a wink. "Does she play center too perhaps?"

"I'm not threatened at all, and yes she does."

"Don't worry Mills. You'll always be our captain," Georgia said patting Millie on the back and hugging her.

Mia felt a bit awkward at first, but it didn't last long. No one liked being the new kid in the group, especially in such a close group like this, but Khloe stuck by her side and introduced her to all the boys from the boy's hockey team.

"So, that's the boy's team. We all grew up together, but we only just recently started hanging out again."

"How come?" Mia asked.

"Well, once it gets colder, there's this pond where we all play. Last season we had a big grudge match, boys versus girls, to settle which team was the best. It was pretty intense. Cameron and Millie weren't talking, and it all turned into a big mess.

That's in the past now though. We're all friends again now. Linkin and Violet are even boyfriend and girlfriend now." Khloe enjoyed playing the tour guide.

"What about Cameron and Millie? They seem pretty close," Mia said, looking over to where Cameron and Millie were splashing each other in the pool.

"Umm, they aren't actually dating, and if you ask them, they're best friends. If you ask me, they're secretly dating! They look like two lovesick puppies."

"Guys and girls, the foods up! Come and get it while it's hot!" Preston's dad shouted from the BBQ area.

"You hungry? I love Preston's BBQs. His mom makes the best burgers. I don't know what she does to them, but they're delicious." Khloe had a one-track mind when it came to good food.

All the kids rushed to the BBQ area and started piling plates with food, though there was no need to rush. There was enough food to feed four teams. The rest of the BBQ settled into the usual flow. The kids hung out in the pool playing Marco Polo and having wrestling matches. The parents hung out in the BBQ area, so they could get a break from all the laughing and screaming.

5

CAMERON WAS WAITING as patiently as he could outside Millie's house for her to finish getting ready. *She's going to have to get a lot faster at doing her hair and getting ready if she expects me to wait outside in the snow every day*, Cameron thought to himself.

Since the big hockey match last year, the two best friends had been walking to school together each school day. It was nice to hang out away from all the other kids and just talk about school, hockey, and lacrosse without the others giggling and making silly jokes.

The walk to school was about a mile, but they never rushed unless it was raining or snowing. If the weather got too cold or wet, then either Cameron's or Millie's parents would drive them.

There were large oak trees that lined most of the streets, so if it was too hot or windy, you could usually shelter under the trees and get some shade while you walked along.

"About time, Mills!" Cameron shouted, cupping his hands together to make his shout even louder as Millie appeared at the large front doorway of her house.

"Please, you've been waiting like two minutes, Cam. Give me a break already. It's the first day of school." The two laughed at each other as Millie walked down the rose-lined front path. It was the usual routine for the two to torment each other. It was all good-hearted fun; not like it had been in the past. Cameron tormented Millie in the morning. She'd torment him right back when she had to wait for him after school while he goofed around with all his buddies.

"So, did you see the new girl at Preston's party?" Millie asked quietly.

"Yep. She seems nice. I didn't get a chance to talk to her though. The girls all reckon she's a good skater. Khloe couldn't shut up about how she tricked her with that first shot on net during practice."

"It was just practice!" Millie blurted out, the

words coming out a little bit more aggressively than she had intended.

"Woah. Settle down. What's up, Mills?"

"It's Mia. What if she takes my spot at center? What if she takes the captain spot away from me?"

"Mills, you need to take a breath and relax. She's just here to fill a spot because Kate left. She didn't plan for Kate to leave, and there's nothing sinister going on. She's not going to take your position at center or the captaincy. You have nothing to worry about. Okay?"

"I know. I'm just being silly. Maybe I just needed someone to set me straight. Thanks, Cam."

"Anytime. You know I always have your back. Always will, Mills."

The rest of the walk left Millie feeling a lot better about Mia. She was just being silly and feeling threatened. It would be good for their team to have another strong player. Maybe the season wouldn't be as hard as they all thought it would?

As Cameron and Millie walked through the large iron gates at the front of the school, Millie could see Mia surrounded by the boys and girls from the hockey teams. Her frown came back. She couldn't seem to shake it, and yet she couldn't help but feel a little sorry for Mia at the same time. All this would be a lot to handle for Mia. First practice, then the pool party, and now the first day of school. It was a big week for anyone let alone someone new to town.

"There's the new girl now," Cameron said to Millie as they headed over to their large group of friends.

"Do you think she needs rescuing? I hope they're not all harassing her with questions."

"She looks okay to me, Mills. Let's go over and say hi."

Mia was used to being the new girl, but this time was a little different.

Both her parents worked in the military. Her father was in the army, and her mother worked as a civilian contractor on military bases. That meant a lot of moving and meeting new people. Most of the schools she went to were attached to the military bases or full of kids just like her. All kids that moved around a lot. Being the new kid in a group of new kids on an army base wasn't anything special. It was just the norm.

Being the new kid in a small town was apparently a much bigger deal.

Cameron and Millie pushed their way through their friends.

"Guys! Enough already. Give Mia some space. Hi, I'm Cameron. We didn't get a chance to meet at the pool party the other day. My friends call me Cam. I'm the captain of the boy's hockey team."

Again, Millie couldn't help but feel a little jealous about the way Cameron was smiling at Mia. You're being silly again, she thought to herself. She was just about to say hello to Mia and the rest of the kids when the bell sounded, announcing homeroom was about to start. Saved by the bell.

The first day at school was always super exciting. You got to find out which of your friends was going to be in your class and what teachers you had.

When Millie walked into her homeroom, she saw she was going to have Sage, Logan, and Rhys in her homeroom with her. She was a little disappointed she didn't have Cameron or Georgia, but there was still a chance she would have one of her other classes with them.

After the first break, Millie was walking down the long corridor to where the lockers were. She noticed Mia was looking up and down the corridor looking a little lost.

"Hey, um, do you need a hand?" Millie asked.

"Well, I, um, yeah. I do. My locker number is forty-five, but I can't find any of the forties?"

"Oh, that's easy. My locker is forty-nine. You're just along from me. The forties are all in the alcove. That's the little hallway just opposite the girl's toilet. Follow me."

The two girls walked along the corridor in silence and turned left into the alcove.

"So, here's mine. That's yours."

"Got it. Thanks for that Millie. I appreciate it," Mia replied, smiling as she unlocked her locker and started putting her books inside.

"No worries. So, how's it going? It can't be easy moving to a new town and starting a new school and stuff?" Millie asked.

"Well, it's going all right, and everyone is being super friendly. I'm used to moving around a lot, but this is different. It's just that I'm not used to having this much attention on me. It's like I'm the only new girl that's ever started and I'm feeling a bit..."

"Overwhelmed?" Millie interrupted her.

"Exactly. Everyone is great, but I've never talked about myself this much in my whole life."

"They are awesome really. They just don't get out a lot. It's such a small town, and most of us all grew up together, so there's not much we don't already know. " Millie said with a laugh. "Look, I'll have a quiet word with the girls and get Cam to mention it to the boys. Make sure they give you some breathing space while you settle in. We sit in the cafeteria at lunch. If you want, you can sit with us."

"Oh, cool. That would be great. Thanks."

"Awesome. I'll see you there then," Millie said, locking her locker and walking away. It wouldn't be fun being the new girl, and Millie knew she had to stop being so weird about the whole thing and make an effort.

"OMG. Sloppy joes on day one. I think the cafeteria must get some sort of deal on this stuff. It's so gross!" Daylyn wrinkled her nose at the plate of food. You couldn't blame her. The sloppy mess running off the side of her bun looked far from appetizing. She pushed it to one side with a disgusted look on her face.

"I like it," Khloe said as she reached over and slid the unwanted sloppy joe onto her own tray. The rest of the girls giggled and laughed.

"Of course, you do, Khloe. You eat everything!" shouted Georgia from the end of the table.

Millie just laughed along with the rest. When she looked up from her tray, she noticed Mia had walked up to their table and was standing there awkwardly, not knowing where to sit.

"Come on guys, make room for Mia." A round of hellos and heys went around the table as all the girls moved over to make some space for Mia. Then, within seconds, the questions started raining down on her.

"So, Mia, do you like sloppy joes?"

"What classes have you got, Mia?"

"Mia, where do you live?"

"Guys! Come on. She just sat down. It's only her first day. Let her have something to eat and breath for five minutes. Jeez."

"Sorry, Mia. We get a bit excited about 'new stuff' around here! We'll let you settle in a little more from now on," Georgia said with a smile.

"Thanks. You've all made me feel super welcome." Mia said quietly.

"So. Who are we playing first again, Millie?" Daylyn asked, changing the subject. The rest of lunch settled into the usual chat about boys and hockey and school. Millie noticed Mia was quiet but was taking part in the conversations some-times. *She didn't look as worried about everything as she had this morning*, Millie thought to her-self. Maybe she had been worrying over nothing after all.

6

"WELL, THAT'S ONE day over and done with!" Cameron shouted as Millie and he walked out of school.

"Yeah, one down and how many left? I think It's a little bit early to be celebrating," Millie laughed.

"Yeah, I know, but we have practice tonight, and I've been waiting all day. Just excited to get back into hockey and out on the ice again."

"Didn't you like field lacrosse?" Millie asked as they crossed the street and turned on to the road that led to her house.

"You know what? I really did. If I could, I would play field lacrosse, and hockey but I just don't have the time. Besides, my mom would probably go nuts driving me all over town three or four nights a week."

"Yep. Dad told me I had to commit to one or the other as well. Field was awesome though. It's nice to be able to play something over summer where you can run around and stuff. Kept all the girls busy. I think next year I'll let someone else have a turn as the lacrosse captain."

"Too much captaincy stuff for you, Mills?"

"Yeah. I love hockey, and it's my life, but it's time to let someone else take over with the lacrosse."

"Yep, it's not easy. Our coach for lacrosse was cool. Coach Nev really knew his stuff."

"That's cool. I watched a few of your practices. He doesn't mind shouting during the games either." Millie said with a laugh.

"Yep, that's him, but he followed up with some great help. He's played lacrosse all his life. The assistant coaches Tyler, Matt, and Jon were cool too. Some of the younger guys really had no idea when we started. They were struggling. By the end of the season, we were starting to really rock it."

"Cool. Good coaches always make it more fun. Anyway, I better get going. You know mom and dad will be waiting," Millie said, mentally facepalming herself.

"They still doing that, huh?" Cameron said with a laugh.

"Every. Year. They take the day off or leave work early and wait for me to come home and ask me how my day went. I keep telling them I'm too old for it, but they don't seem to care."

"It's adorable, Mills," Cameron said, laughing harder now.

"It's something all right. Anyways, Cam, I'll see you tomorrow."

"See you later, Mills," Cameron said, waving as he walked away up the road still smiling.

"Welcome home, sweetie!" Millie's parents shouted as she walked in the front door.

"Seriously you guys, I'm getting a bit old for this," Millie said, trying as hard as she could to look sternly at her parents and look a lot older than she was.

"Never too old. We'll be doing this when you first start college. Might even wait in your dorm room! So, how was school?" Millie's mom asked as she sat down with a plate of biscuits and muffins.

"Good," Millie replied with a mouthful of blue-berry muffin.

"Just good?" her dad asked. "You have to give us something more than 'good' Mills."

"Dad, it was fantastic! All the kids were swell, and I learned a bunch. Gee whiz, I wish it could have lasted longer!" Millie said with a big, exaggerated smile on her face.

"I do believe that's sarcasm, dear. Maybe we should homeschool her?"

"Mom! I was joking! No homeschool."

"See, we can do jokes too, miss! Okay, we get it you're getting older, but you're still our little girl. Did you get any homework?"

"No, mom. Not the first day. What's for dinner?" Millie couldn't smell anything cooking, which was unusual. Her mom loved to cook.

"Well, we decided to take it easy on the first day of school too. Your mom deserves a break, so I suggested we head out for dinner. You happy to go out for a burger and a shake?"

"Thanks, guys. That's awesome! It looks like today didn't turn out too bad after all." Millie said with a smile.

"I heard Mia is an awesome hockey player," Linkin

said, slipping his shoulder pads on. The boys were all sitting in the change room putting their hockey gear on.

"Oh, you heard huh? Let me guess who you heard that from...Violet," Hunter said, rolling his eyes. Violet was Linkin's girlfriend, and they both loved gossiping about the teams to each other. If you wanted to know something about any of the boys or girls from the hockey team, you talked to Linkin or Violet.

"Maybe," Linkin said laughing.

"Linkin, if any of the guys on the team had a secret, Violet would be the first to know," Cameron said from the other side of the change room. "If I ever have a secret we want to keep from the girls, I'll be sure to leave you out! Speaking of secrets, how did the girls always seem to know what plays and lines we were going to play before we played them?"

"Cam, firstly, I wouldn't tell them team secrets. Secondly, we don't have that many plays, and we always have the same players. It's not rocket science. Anyway. So, apparently that new girl Mia is a pretty wicked skater. Maybe even better than Millie. Millie won't be liking that at all."

"No, she's not!" Cameron didn't mean it to come

out like that. All the chatter in the change room stopped as the guys turned to look at Cameron.

"Woah! I didn't mean anything by it." Linkin looked a little hurt.

"Sorry. I mean, I haven't seen her play yet. Mills didn't say anything much to me either. Not that I would tell you all if she had."

"All right. Guess we'll see when we watch the girls play, huh?" Hunter replied as he finished doing up his skates. "Well, is everyone ready to practice? Last one out is cleaning the change room at the end of practice!" There was a mad rush to throw on gear and get out the door. No one wanted to be the guy that had to stay behind and hang up all the sweaty jerseys. Gross!

"Mia, stop playing with your peas," Mia's dad said.

"Sorry. It was a big day, and I'm really not that hungry."

"Meatball, what's wrong?" Mia's mom asked.

"Mom. You know I hate that nickname. Nothing is wrong. I'm just really tired. Today actually went a lot better than I thought it would. The girls from the hockey team are super friendly, and my teachers are nice."

"Well, that's good honey. I'm glad you had a good day. When is your next hockey practice?" her dad asked.

"It was supposed to be tomorrow night, but Coach Phil said they scheduled an exhibition match with a team from the next town over. So, we're not having practice now. Just playing instead."

"That's good, give you a chance to show them what you're made of."

"Yep. I would have liked a few more practices, but games are fun too." Mia knew she was a little rusty on the skates, but a game against another team would be better than practice to get her sorted.

"You have any homework, dear?" Mia's mom asked.

"No, mom, not the first day. I'm full. Can I please go and watch some YouTube videos in my room?"

"Sure, Meatball. Just clean the table off first," her dad replied with a smile.

"Dad! Stop it! Okay, thanks. Dinner was great mom!" Mia said as she stood and started cleaning the table.

"You're welcome, honey. I'm glad you enjoyed

your first day. Leave the rest. Your father can help me."

"Thanks, mom! You're the best!" Mia replied as she ran out of the dining room before her mom changed her mind and her dad could say anything.

"Oh, great! First day of school 'chores pass' huh, Meatball? Enjoy it while it lasts," her dad said as he stood up to start cleaning the dishes. Mia just laughed as she ran upstairs to her room. Not a bad first day at all.

7

"ARE YOU SERIOUS coach?" Millie asked, sounding upset.

"Afraid so, girls. Their coach just called me. Apparently, the bus bringing the team from school broke down on the highway. So, that meant they had to cancel. Nothing we can do about it now."

A loud chorus of groans and grumbles went up around the changeroom. Now what were they all going to do? No team to play meant they would have to have boring old practice now. They really needed this pre-season warm-up game to see where they were really at.

"Coach, um, the boys are practicing now too, right? On the other rink, right?" Khloe asked.

"Umm, yeah. Why, Khloe?"

"Could we ask them to scrimmage? A boys versus girls match for old time's sake?"

"Yeah, coach, can we?"

"That would be so cool! Coach Phil, can we?" All the girls chimed in.

"Okay! Okay, I surrender!" Coach Phil shouted, raising his hands in mock surrender. "I'll go and ask Coach John right now. Jeez. Finish getting ready, and I'll see what I can do, okay? No promises though, and no complaining or sulking if they say no."

Coach Phil wondered who was really in charge around here as he walked out of the changeroom and headed to where the boys were getting ready. He'd never intended on coaching this long after his daughter moved up a few years ago, but this group of girls was really a great bunch of kids, and his daughter's team had already had a coach.

"Hey John, look we've got a bit of a problem, and the girls and I were thinking that you might be able to help us out."

"Sure, Phil. What's up?"

"Well, the team that was coming to play us tonight canceled five minutes ago. The girls were all pumped up to play a game, and we were hoping your team might be interested in a boys versus girls match? The referees are already here as well. It would be great to get an extra game in before the tournament," Coach Phil explained as the boys started drifting out of the changeroom and gathering around the two coaches.

"Well, I'd love to help you out and all, but I have a few things I'd really like to nail down before the boys..."

"Coach, please, can we? The last time we played them on the pond, it was awesome. It would be nice to do it again," Cameron said while all the other boys stood around nodding in agreement.

"Yeah, coach! We can practice some of those new plays you wanted to teach us," Logan, Millie's cousin, said as he squeezed his head into his large goalie helmet.

"All right, all right. Hey, Phil, are your girls as bossy as this lot?" John asked as the two coaches walked out of the change room. Phil laughed loudly, shaking his head as the two coaches walked away from the group of boys.

"I wish they were only as bossy as your boys, John. Sometimes I feel like they're the coaches and I'm just along for the ride! See you out on the ice in five minutes!" Coach Phil said as he walked back towards the girl's change room to give them the good news.

"Are you guys ready for a game?" Cameron shouted to the boys after the coaches left.

"1, 2, 3, Lightning!" chorused the boys, as they banged their sticks against the benches. The sound of their cheers rumbled around the arena. *Guess they're as ready as they'd ever be*, Coach John thought to himself.

"You hear that?" Georgia asked from inside the girl's change room as Coach Phil walked in.

"They all sound pretty excited for a team that's about to lose!" Khloe said giggling.

"Now, now girls. Let's not get overconfident. We've got a whole game ahead of us. Finish getting your gear on, and I'll see you out on the ice. Millie, can you take them through the cheer?"

"Hurricanes, Hurricanes, who are we?" Millie shouted.

"We're the team that they all want to be!" the girls all shouted back.

"Hurricanes, Hurricanes, what do you say?" Millie yelled back.

"Stand back, stand back! We are here to play!" Now they were ready.

"Hurricanes!" They all shouted while jumping up and down.

The game started off like most hockey games, with each team carefully trying to feel each other out and check for any weak spots in the other's game. *Damn, the boys were getting better*, Millie thought as she slammed through the door and onto the bench. They hadn't gotten anywhere yet.

"Mills, I'm going to have a heart attack," Georgia panted as she grabbed for her water bottle.

"Us, too!" chorused the twins, Daylyn and Ashlyn, from the other end of the bench. They were getting the workout of their lives on defense. For two girls that played hockey like they could read each other's minds, that was saying something.

Just then, the buzzer sounded to signal the end of the first period, with the scores still tied at zero. *At least they could catch their breath*, Millie thought to herself as her teammates came off the ice.

"Cam, come on! We need you to kick it into a

higher gear, buddy." Coach John said as soon as they were all huddled up together on the ice. "I always thought they were good, but they're bringing their 'A' game tonight, boys. Whoever the new girl is, she's good. It doesn't seem to matter which line we get. They're not letting up on the pressure. I need everyone to kick it up in the next period, and we'll try and get a score on the board."

In the girl's huddle, Coach Phil was giving a similar speech to the girl's team.

"The pressure is amazing, but you need to keep it up for another two periods. So, quick shifts and don't get caught with bad changes. Defense, keep pushing them out in front of the net. Forwards, we need you to keep moving the puck around as much as possible and make sure you're looking for the girl in front of the net. They're bigger than most of you guys, but we have the speed and the skills. It's making them tired. If I had to guess, they're going to be gassed by the start of the third. Great job, all of you! All right, let's get back out there!"

Millie was tired. So tired. The first game of the season and she was starting to realize just how out of game shape she really was. Lacrosse had been great, but hockey fit was something entirely different. She looked over at Mia as she skated out to face off against Cam. She didn't look tired at all! Did Cam just smile at her?

"Are they serious?" she said under her breath, her eyes narrowing.

"What, Mills?" Coach Phil asked.

Millie had found the motivation to get her through the rest of the game.

"Nothing, Coach." Nothing at all.

The second period didn't change the score-board much. Both teams kept battling through each shift looking for that first goal. The boys were stronger than most of the girls, but the girls were quicker than most of the boys, so they couldn't just use their strength against the girls, and it was starting to show. Shots were a little slower, passes were just a bit wider, and players took a fraction of a second longer to react.

At the start of the third period, the score was still 0-0. The first team to score now might just be the winners with no time left to come back.

Millie was facing off against Cameron. Her eyes narrowed. Her jaw set. Cameron raised his eye-brows questioningly.

"Mils, you ready...to lose...?" he said between breaths.

"Please. Don't even bother. You're too tired to talk! If you give up now, I'll let you score a goal!" Millie shot back at him.

Cam was tired. Seriously tired, but he couldn't work out why Millie looked so angry. Sure, she sounded like she was joking around, but that scowl and angry expression looked far from happy.

"Bring it, Mills. I can do this all night long!" Cam shot back.

The buzzer sounded, and the ref blew her whistle and dropped the puck. The third period was underway!

The slugging match continued almost all the way through the third period, and with only a few minutes left on the clock, Cameron and Millie found themselves facing off against each other again.

"Ready, Cam?" Millie asked, puffing. She was too tired to be angry at Cam now.

"Ready...as I'll...ever be." Cameron said quietly back. It hurt too much to talk. The ref blew his whistle and dropped the puck.

Mills pulled the puck back and quickly took

off to Cam's right, only to have herself heading straight into "The Wall," which is what they called Linkin and Ben, The Lightening's best defensive line. She had the speed though, so she was able to push them over their blue line and could hear her teammate's calling close behind her. As she went towards the boards to get the puck deeper into their end, Ben managed to poke her stick and Ben was able to grab the puck.

"Better luck next time!" Ben shouted to Mills, passing the puck to Cameron, who was now sailing back up the ice with only Daylyn in his way. The rest of the girls hadn't expected the quick turnover and were all racing back. Daylyn was watching Cam and trying to read where he would go. He feinted quickly to the left, which had her shift with him, but by the time she recovered, he had already pushed past on her right side. Cameron pulled on the last of his energy reserves and knuckled down for a final drive on the goal.

Khloe was out of the net at the top of the goalie crease, shuffling backward, her head swiveling from side to side as she watched Cam's stick move. He was slipping the puck back and forth in front of him.

"Oh boy, oh boy, oh boy," Khloe whispered quietly to herself. This was the ultimate challenge for any goalie. One-on-one, no defense, no offense. Just the goalie and the opposing player facing off. No one to blame but herself if she mucked this up.

"Shoot! Shoot ,Cam!" Coach John was shouting from the bench, his teammates banging their sticks on the boards as they all stood up.

Cam pulled his hockey stick back, and with a powerful swing, sent the puck hurtling towards the top right corner of the net. It was a massive shot, the puck screaming through the air. *There was no way Khloe was going to stop it*, Cam thought.

Smack! The puck bounced off Khloe's stick and spiraled away over the net, bouncing off the boards and sliding around. Ashlyn grabbed it and sent up the ice to Georgia, who was looking for Millie or Lola. Georgia managed to get it into the boys' end and dumped the puck around the boards. Lola and Linkin were battling in the corner. Lola flipped the puck over Linkin's stick, and Millie did a one-timer. The shot was quick but not quick enough for Logan, who caught it in his glove. Both teams did a quick change.

Preston won the face off and passed it quickly up the board to Rhys. Rhys took off down the boards, and he quickly looked and saw Preston and Reid were right with him. He went deep and saw them both heading to the net, but then he saw Taylor ready for a shot from the point. He sent the puck back and Taylor took a slapshot. It went flying in but was deflected towards the boards. Sage took her chance to change and raced to the bench. Mia jumped on the ice, and Taylor hadn't noticed Mia was now behind him. Keira saw her chance and sent the puck sailing right in between Taylor and Clay to Mia's stick.

By the time both boys reacted, they realized they were in a lot of trouble. Big trouble.

Mia took off towards Logan, who was already out of his net and ready for her.

Now it was the girls' turn to scream as the whole team stood on the benches.

Logan was sweating so hard the sweat was leaking through the skull-head bandana he wore under his goalie helmet. It was his lucky bandana. He never played without it. The new girl was barreling down on him so fast it was as if she was being chased by a pack of wild dogs! Wow, she was fast!

Mia had watched Cam's shot on goal and had been studying Logan as he saved shots all night. She knew he was fast—*maybe a little too fast*, she thought as she quickly came up with an idea. *Yep, she thought to herself; it might just work.*

Logan was watching Mia's stick. He knew she liked shooting from the right, and liked to go up top, and was ready for her shot. Mia was only a few meters from the crease when she pulled her shoulder around and got ready to shoot.

Logan saw the move, and his brain told him everything he needed to know. His reflexes kicked in, and he dived to the left, creating a wall. The only thing was, Mia wasn't there! She'd slowed and ducked to her left, flicking the puck over his stretched-out legs, almost in slow-motion. He didn't even need to look. The cheers from the girls' bench told him everything he needed to know.

The buzzer blew. The girls flooded out from their bench as they all piled on Mia and Khloe in the center of the ice.

"Good game!" Coach John yelled to Coach Phil as the two headed out on the ice for the handshakes.

"Thanks, the girls did it all!" Coach Phil laughed as all the players lined up to shake hands. What an epic game!

After practice, Cameron's dad picked Millie and Cameron up. Millie was crashing at their house tonight. Millie's parents were going for a long-awaited date night in the city, and they were going to stay over instead of driving home.

"Thanks for picking us up, Ryan, and thanks for letting me stay over," Millie said as they both piled into the back of Cameron's dad's police cruiser. Cameron's dad was a local police officer, and he didn't get to come to many practices or games because of his work. It was usually Cam's mom who picked him up and watched him play.

"Yeah, thanks, dad. I'm glad you got to see a game," Cam joined in. His dad had an important job, and Cameron was proud his dad helped protect people in the town, even if it meant he had to work a lot. One day, he hoped to get a job in law enforcement too, just like his dad. Not as a police officer, though. He had always dreamed of becoming an FBI agent.

"No problem, guys. I'll tell the chief an animal died in the cruiser. It might explain that terrible smell in the back."

Both Cameron and Millie couldn't help but giggle. They really did stink!

After they showered and headed to bed, they both lay in bed talking and laughing. Cameron had a bunk bed in his room, so Millie always got the top bunk when she stayed over. It wasn't unusual for the two of them to talk for hours about hockey, school, and their friends.

"You guys are going to dominate this year, Mills," Cameron said, followed by a loud yawn. He was exhausted. "Mills?" Cameron said.

What he got in reply was the tiniest little snore. Cameron couldn't help but smile. Millie had fallen asleep in the middle of their conversation.

"Night, Mills," Cameron said, rolling over and pulling the covers up to his chin. Within a few minutes, Millie's snores were joined by Cameron's much louder snoring as the two fell fast asleep.

8

"OMG, what a game," Khloe said for about the tenth time. The group of friends was gathered around the large oak tree outside the school. The weather was a little cooler this time of year but not cold enough to force them into school a minute earlier than necessary.

"Khloe, seriously, I think we've heard enough about the game." Logan rolled his eyes, looking around for some support from the rest of the boys. It was no surprise after their 1-0 loss to the girls that most of the boys just wanted to forget it and move on.

"All the way to school, it's all I got. 'Hey, you remember when we beat you at hockey?' or my all-time, personal favorite, 'Remember when I saved all those goals, but you let that goal in?' Seriously. From one goalie to another, where's the professional courtesy?" Logan was pretty bummed out about the game and could usually take some teasing as well as the next guy, but, it, well, it just sucked.

"Okay, Logan. I'll give you a break," Khloe said, laughing. But she looked around at the group of friends with a wink, which Logan couldn't see. "Unlike Mia, who popped that puck over your leg!"

"That's it. I'm not talking to you anymore," Logan said, sticking his bottom lip out and narrowing his eyes.

"What are you drawing, Ben?" Lola asked, standing up to peek over his shoulder.

"It's Logan lying down while Mia scores on him."

"Ben! Whose side are you on man? Geez!" Logan blurted out.

"Sorry, dude," Ben said cracking up. He carefully tore the page out of his artbook and handed it to Mia. "Here, Mia, this is for you," Ben said as he handed over the drawing.

"Wow! That's so cool. I didn't know you were so good at drawing," Mia said.

"Well, I'm okay, but Lola is heaps better than me."

"What's going on, guys?" Cameron asked as he and Millie walked up to where everyone was sitting.

"Just the usual, Cam," Luke replied. Luke was Cameron's best friend and had been playing right wing on the line alongside him for as long as he could remember. Luke could still remember the first time they met each other at house league. "Khloe teased Logan about how he sucked the other night. Ben drew a picture of how Logan sucked the other night. Oh, and Logan, you sucked the other night!" Luke laughing.

"That's it. I'm done. I'm going inside." Logan stood up and started to huff and puff, walking towards the front doors of the school.

"Logan, wait!" Cameron shout.

"Yeah, Logan, wait a minute. We just got here!" Millie shouted. Logan stopped in his tracks and turned around.

"We didn't get a chance to thank you for sucking the other night!" Millie blurted out.

"Yeah, thanks, bro!" Cameron chimed in.

"Ahh! You...I'll...bah!" Logan stormed away while all the kids laughed and cried hysterically, rolling around on the ground.

"Will he be okay?" Mia said wiping a tear away, still trying to get her giggling under control.

"Oh, yeah. We do this every time we lose. He

knows we love him, and really, we could have scored," Cameron said as the bell sounded to signal the start of another school day.

"Hey, Mia! How was English?" Cameron asked as he walked from one class to another.

"Oh, um, hey, Cameron. English was good. It's not my favorite class, but the teacher is nice," Mia replied, blushing a little. *Seriously, girl, get it together already*, she thought.

"Hey, it's just Cam to my friends, Mia. Yeah, English isn't my fav class either. What's your next class?"

"Let me look," Mia said, pulling her class schedule out of her pocket and unfolding it. "Oh, it's math."

"Cool, me too. I'll walk with you." Cameron said to her as the two of them turned and walked down the long hallway towards the math classroom. Just as they got to the large doors, a kid came bursting out of the door, bumping into Mia and knocking her into Cameron, her books spilling onto the floor.

"Watch it, dude!" Cameron shouted, putting a

hand out to steady Mia. It was at that moment that Millie, who was walking down the other hallway, glimpsed Cam and Mia through the swinging door. She saw him put his hand out and touch Mia just before the door swung shut again. *What the heck?* Millie thought to herself, picking up the pace to try and reach the door as fast as she could.

"Sorry!" The kid shouted back, not slowing as he continued going full pace down the hall.

"Are you okay?" Cameron asked Mia, kneeling and helping her to pick up her spilled books and papers.

"Yeah, I'm okay, it was nothing. Thanks..." Mia started to say before the door swung open again, nearly knocking the pair over.

"What's going on?" Millie blurted out, looking down at Cameron and Mia kneeling down on the tiles.

"Oh hey, Mills, nothing much. I...I was just...just helping Mia pick up her books," Cam stuttered. "Some jerk almost knocked us over. You want to walk with us?"

"No. I mean, I can't. I'm going in the opposite direction." Millie said, a harsh tone creeping into her voice.

"Well, I'll see you after school then?" Cam asked as he stood up.

"I can't, sorry. I said I'd hang out with Georgia tonight before practice." Millie said as she started to walk away.

"Oh, okay. Well, I'll talk to you later, Mills."

"Yep. See you both later," Millie threw out over her shoulder, not bothering to turn around.

"Did I do something wrong?" Mia asked Cameron as Millie walked away.

"No, no you didn't. Mills is dealing with something. Don't even worry about it. Let's get to class before we're late." Cameron didn't understand what Millie's problem was lately. Why couldn't she just be chill like Mia? *Girls were hard work*, he thought to himself. One day he'd figure them out.

9

"All right everybody, settle down. You know what's coming up next week." Coach Phil said to the players and parents sitting around the large conference room at the arena. The girls and boys had both just finished big practice sessions and were looking worn out. It was the perfect time for the team meeting as they had all burned off any extra energy and would pay more attention.

The two teams were meeting together as they were in the same age group. There were too many teams to have all the Dakota teams meet at the same time, so they split up after each practice session.

"Now, I know you've all been giving it a hundred percent, but..."

"It's time for 110%!" Georgia shouted out. Most

of the girls giggled, and even a few of the boys joined in. Apparently, they weren't as worn out as Coach Phil has assumed.

"Thanks, Georgia. Yes, 110%. Apparently, I need to start mixing up my 'motivational' speeches a bit more. As I was saying, the yearly Dakota Town Tournament is coming up, and I'd like to win it. As the home team, we need to set the tone early for the tournament, and that's going to involve all the players helping out."

"Coach Phil is right everyone," Coach John, the boy's coach, joined in. "We expect you to not only show up at practice and games but also help run the tournament as well. As you all know, tournaments aren't cheap, and we rely on parents and kids to help out as much as possible."

"Yes, and that means you're all going to be volunteering. Each age group is responsible for certain volunteer activities during the tournament. For my girls, that's going to be the 50-50 raffle tickets." Coach Phil said looking to where most of the girls were sitting. "You girls are going to sweet talk all the parents and friends to help us sell a record amount of 50-50 tickets this year. I'll even throw in a prize to the pair of girls that sell the most as a little incentive!" The girls glanced

at each other, mentally choosing who they would pair up with even before Coach Phil had finished.

There was nothing like a little healthy competition to help motivate highly competitive kids to go the extra mile, Coach Phil thought as he saw the looks passing between the girls, and he already knew the record was in the bag this year.

"And for the boys, have I got a job for you!" Coach John shouted. "Boys, you'll be running the gate and helping out as timekeepers and scorers." The boys started to grumble and looked disappointed. "Yeah, I know, it's not fair the girls get a prize for selling the most 50-50 tickets and you don't. So, to make it fair, I'm going to offer two mystery prizes myself. Every time you volunteer for gate duty, or whatever, I'll put your name in a hat. The more you do, the more entries you get." The frowns on the boys faces quickly switched to grins. Oh, it was on now!

"Thanks, coaches. Okay, for those that don't know me, my name is Chris, and I'm the league convenor for Dakota. I'd just like to say thanks to both the girls' team and the boys' team, and the parents, for helping us out this year. It's you guys and girls that help make the tournament a success each year. I'm going to announce the first games for the tournament now, so you can all get home and have a shower. You stink!" Chris said with a wink that made all the kids in the room laugh and look around at each other.

"Anyway, let's get down to business. I only have the Friday night games at this point. The rest will be sent out tomorrow. Hurricanes, your first game is against the Smithton Seahawks on Friday night at 8:00 pm." The girls all smiled and nodded, looking around the room at each other. *Easy first game for them*, they were all thinking to themselves. The Seahawks finished last in our division last year.

"Lighting, you're going to be playing the East London Flyers at 6:00 pm. Both games will be played out of this arena." Cameron shook his head, and Hunter audibly groaned. The rest of the boys had worried looks on their faces. The Flyers were the toughest team in their league, and losing to them straight away could mean the difference between an easy tournament run and fighting their way through all the teams.

"Each team plays once on Friday night and twice on Saturday, with the top four teams moving onto the semifinals and finals Sunday. We're running the tournament out of two arenas, but your games will all be out of this one. It's going to be packed all weekend, so make sure you allow a few minutes extra for parking. That's it from me. Good luck to you all, and thanks again to all the volunteers. This is the first tournament of the year and is going to set the bar high for all the other teams. Oh, it's also a qualifier for the state championships at the end of the season, so play your hearts out kids!" The parents clapped as Chris took a seat next to the two coaches.

"Thanks, Chris. I know how busy you are, and we appreciate you giving us a heads-up about Friday night's games. Okay, Coach John, do you have anything to add?" Coach Phil asked.

"No, my boys are good to go whenever the meeting is done," Coach John replied, giving Phil a thumbs up.

"All right. Now for the serious stuff," Coach Phil said with a wink. "We want all the kids to be at the arena and ready at their assigned dressing room at least one hour before their scheduled game. We'll have a quick chat then a warm-up before dressing for the game. If you're late, you'll sit. Now, remember, this is the Dakota tournament, and we're going to win it! So, bring your 'A' game!" All the kids clapped and cheered. Spirits were running high throughout the room.

"All right, all right. Everyone have a good night, and we'll see you all fresh next Friday night."

Millie was lying in bed watching Netflix on her iPad when she saw an instant message from Cam pops up on the screen.

You awake, Mills?

Yeah, just watching Netflix. What's up?

You guys got an awesome draw for Friday.

Thanks! Yeah, tough break for you boys.

'Rolls eyes,' you don't have to tell me! The Flyers are good. Real good. Every game we played last season was tough. Anyway, I missed walking home with you tonight.

Yeah, sorry. I missed walking home with you too, but I promised I'd hang with Georgia and have some bestie time.

Ah, that's okay. Anyway, mom said I gotta go to bed, but I'll see you in the morning, right?

Ah, okay. Yep, I'll see you in the morning!

Night, Mills!

Night Cam! See you tomorrow.

Millie turned her iPad off and plugged it into the charger beside her bed. She couldn't help but think about how she had reacted earlier in the day when she saw Cam with Mia. Every time she thought she had her feelings and thoughts about Cameron and Mia under control, she'd go all weird again. *Get it together girl!* she thought to herself as she pulled the covers up and got comfortable. He's your best friend, not your boyfriend.

10

THE NEXT NIGHT the boys were all lined up together against the cold glass of the arena watching as the girls' team finished their practice and slowly started to filter off the ice towards their change room.

"Still can't believe the girls beat us," Preston grumbled under his breath as the girls all left the ice.

"Well, if you played as hard as you talked, then we would have won!" Hunter shot straight back at him. The rest of the boys all laughed and snickered.

"All right, everyone out on the ice!" Coach John yelled, breaking up the laughter. Great, he thought to himself, it was going to be one of 'those' practices.

"I still can't believe we were that lucky for once with the tournament draw," Georgia said as she sat down next to Millie and Khloe on the bench. "We're never that lucky!" she said as she started undoing the laces on her skates.

"Please, Georgia, that team may have finished on the bottom of the league last season, but that was last season. This is this season. Anything could have happened since then," Lola said from the opposite side of the dressing room. All the girls stopped their chatter for a minute and turned to look at where Lola was sitting.

"Um, that's the most I've heard you say all week," Khloe blurted out, giggling. The other girls laughed, and Lola blushed.

"She's right, though, you know. We shouldn't just assume that just because they were terrible last year that they're going to be terrible again this year. Look at us, we were good this year, but now we have Mia to help us. We're going to be even better," Millie said softly.

"Thanks," Mia said quietly. Millie nodded and smiled.

"You're welcome." Millie wished she could see

past these uneasy feelings she'd been having about Cam and Mia and be friendlier, but whenever she thought the feelings were gone, they'd come flooding back.

"Okay, I'm heading home. I'll see you all later," Sage called as she headed out the door.

"We're off too," Daylyn and Ashlyn, the twins, replied in unison. The girls all said goodbye to each other as they started to filter out of the change room one after the other.

As Millie left the change room, she looked over to where the boys were playing and noticed Mia had walked over to the stand and was sitting watching the boys' practice. Millie was about to go over and ask her if she needed a ride home when she noticed Mia waving to someone out on the ice. Millie looked and saw Cameron had skated by the glass and waved back to her.

Millie turned and started to walk out the doors towards the carpark where she knew her mother would be waiting in the car for her.

"Good practice, honey?" her mom asked as she got in the car.

"Yeah," Millie replied quietly.

"You okay, Mills?" her mom asked.

"Yeah, mom, just tired. Can we go home?"

"Sure, honey. We'll get you home and into the shower."

"Oooohhh, someone has a girlfriend!" Hunter shouted as he skated past Cameron.

"Shut up!" Cameron shouted skating away from the ice. Cameron didn't know why, but there was just something about Mia that made him feel good.

"Admit it, bro. You dig Mia," Luke said as he skated alongside his best friend.

"She is cute," Cameron said, glancing again over to where Mia sat on the stands.

"Well, what's the problem then? Ask her out already. We've all seen you staring."

"It's not that easy, what about..."

"Mills? She's your best friend, Cam. She'll understand. Talk to her about it, but don't keep putting off talking to Mia. You'll only regret it." Luke said as he skated off towards where the rest of the team was grabbing a drink from the boards.

Cameron felt torn, but obviously he hadn't been hiding his feelings as well as he thought he had.

Cameron made up his mind as he started to skate towards the rest of his team. He'd talk to Millie and let her know how he felt.

Mia didn't mind that her mom was late. It gave her a chance to watch Cameron out on the ice. When he skated past where she was sitting, she smiled and gave a small, hesitant wave. Cameron smiled and waved back, taking his eye off the puck for a moment. One of the other boys, Preston she thought, swooped in and took the puck from him. She could see the rest of the boys laughing and looking towards where she was sitting.

"Cameron! Earth to Cameron! Are we going to be joining in with the rest of the team for practice tonight?" Mia heard Coach John shout out on the ice.

Mia couldn't help but giggle as Cam rolled his eyes, gave her a small nod, and skated off to the other side of the ice. *He really is cute*, she thought.

"Mia!" her mom shouted loudly from the door, causing Mia to jump. "Are you coming or what? I haven't got all night, Meatball."

"Mia Meatball, huh?" Rhys said as he walked

towards the toilet, past where Mia and her mom were standing.

"Mom! I told you I hated that name, and now Rhys knows too! You're so embarrassing!" Mia said as she felt her face flush hotly.

"Don't worry, Meatball. I won't tell anyone," Rhys said with a huge smile on his face as he bowed dramatically. "Your secret is safe with me!"

"Thanks, Rhys," Mia said as she started walking away with her mom.

"Until I get back from the toilet that is!" Rhys said laughing hysterically.

"Mom! See! Oh, I—never mind!" Mia said as she stormed off towards the exit. *Kids*, her mom thought, *there was never a dull moment.*

Millie was laying in bed when she saw her iPad light up. She looked at it for several minutes, not really wanting to pick it up. Eventually, her curiosity got the better of her, and she reached for the iPad.

Mills, are you up?

Yeah, just lying here trying to sleep.

Ah, okay, sorry.

Cam?

Yeah, Mills?

Ask her out. She's really cute and super nice, and I know she has a crush on you.

Wait, I, um, I don't know what to say. How did you know?

I'm not silly. You're best my best friend, Cam. She's lucky to have you. Now, stop wasting time and ask her out already before someone else does.

Thanks, Mills. You're the best.

I know. Now, I need to go to sleep. I'm super tired. Text her and I will see you in the morning.

Thanks, Mills! Night.

Night, Cam. See you tomorrow. Good luck!

Millie felt like a weight had been lifted off her chest. She knew Mia and Cam would be good together, and she didn't feel guilty or sad about it anymore. Things would change between her and Cam, but they'd always be best friends.

Mia was lying in bed watching YouTube when a message popped up on her screen from a number she didn't recognize.

Hey, is this Mia?

Who's this?

Oh, hey, it's Cameron. You know, from school?

Mia felt like she was going to throw up. OMG! How did Cameron get her number? Was this a joke? Mia's mind was running a hundred miles an hour with all sorts of random thoughts shooting through her head.

Oh hey, hello. How'd you get my number?

Mills gave it to me. I hope that's okay? You weren't sleeping, were you?

No, and yeah that's cool. What's up?

Look, I, do you want to go out?

> Like somewhere?

**No, well, yes, I mean like boyfriend
and girlfriend.**

Mia's was so shocked her phone slipped out of
her hand and fell onto the floor with a loud bang.
She was scrambling around looking for it in the
dark when she saw the screen flash with another
message from Millie.

**Do it already. He's really nice, and you
two will be cute together.**

> You don't mind? I thought you might
> be upset. How did you know I even
> liked him?

**We aren't blind, silly. We could all see.
He's my best friend. I know you'll be good
for him.**

> Thanks, Millie.

**My friends call me, Mills. I'll talk to you
tomorrow Meatball!**

Mia couldn't believe how her night had turned
out. She hated that everyone knew her nickname

now, but—OMG!—Cam had asked her out! Oh no! She hadn't messaged Cam back!

Cam?

Yeah, Mia?

Yes, I will be your girlfriend.

Sweet!!! I gotta go now. My dad just shouted at me, but I'll see you at school tomorrow?

Yes, for sure! I can't wait! Night Cam!

Night, Meatball!

Seriously? Everyone knew? *Oh well*, Mia thought to herself as she slipped her phone back onto the bedside table. Suddenly she couldn't wait to get to sleep and go to school tomorrow. Dakota was turning out to be the best town ever!

11

MILLIE THOUGHT IT would have been awkward as she and Cameron walked to school, but if anything, she felt better than she had in weeks. It was as if a weight had been lifted from her.

"Oh, so you'll probably want to walk with Mia from now on then, Cam?" Millie teased as they walked along the road towards school.

Cameron just laughed.

"No, I'll always walk with you, Mills. Besides, she lives on the other side of town. I'd have to leave home at least an hour earlier! That would suck," Cameron shot straight back.

The two of them continued to walk along together towards school, teasing each other back and forth, just like old times. Before long, they turned the final corner and could see the large front gates of the school.

Cameron was getting more nervous the closer they got to school. It was one thing to talk to Mia through text, but in person was completely different. Millie could sense Cameron tensing up beside her.

"You'll be fine, silly. Just calm down. You look like you're about to vomit!" Millie laughed hysterically.

"Stop it, Mills!" Cameron said. He did feel a little queasy all of a sudden.

"Just go up to her and say hello, then hold her hand. If you don't make it a big deal, none of the others will."

"Oh, they will. Don't doubt it."

Cameron took a deep breath and headed over towards where Mia was standing and talking with Georgia, Violet, Hunter, and Luke.

"Hey, Cam, what's going on?" Hunter asked as Cameron stopped walking and stood next to Mia and Georgia.

"Not much. Hey, Mia, Georgia, Violet. Hey, Mia, have you got a second?" Cameron asked motioning away from the group.

"Sure," Mia said as she followed Cam a little ways away from the group of friends.

"What gives, Mills?" Georgia asked, glancing over to where Cameron and Mia were talking. Before Millie could say a word, Cameron hesitantly reached out and took Mia's hand.

"Whoa!" Hunter exclaimed loudly enough for everyone, including Mia and Cameron, to hear. Mia didn't turn and look, but judging by the red blush spreading across her face, she had heard. There was a lot of giggling and whispering amongst the group before a glare from Cameron silenced most of the boys.

"Enough, guys, leave them alone," Millie said to the girls that were still whispering and giggling. The bell sounded, signaling the beginning of class, saving both Cameron and Mia from any more teasing.

Cameron said goodbye to Mia and headed off with Luke and Hunter towards homeroom.

Mia headed off with Georgia towards their homeroom, and no sooner had they turned the corner out of eyesight and earshot of the rest of the group, that Georgia was all over her.

"OMG, Mia! You have to tell me everything! How did this happen? Is Mills okay with it? OMG, this

is all happening too fast!" Georgia started firing questions off left and right, her mouth moving faster than her brain until it all ended up in a jumbled rush of words. Mia giggled, still blushing, but she'd started to calm down. She didn't like being the center of attention, but she had expected this reaction, which made it a little easier to handle.

"Well, um, he messaged me last night and it just sort of happened. Millie messaged me too, and we talked, and she's cool with it. That's about it."

"No way! That's the worst story I ever heard. Anyway, sleepover at my place tonight. All the girls will be there, and I'm not taking no for an answer." Georgia said excitedly, linking her arm through Mia's as they walked along the hall.

"Mia, Georgia! We're over here," Millie said, calling out to the two girls as they walked out of class at lunchtime.

"Hey, Mills, what's going on?" Georgia asked as they sat down in the circle of girls.

"Well, we're talking about the sleepover and some other stuff," Khloe answered.

"Mostly about Mia Meatball and her new

boyfriend!" Daylyn and Ashlyn blurted out in unison. This set all the girls giggling and laughing.

"So, everybody is okay for tonight?" Georgia asked.

"Well, I have to check with my mom and dad, but they'll be cool," Mia answered.

"Awesome. It'll be super fun. My mom and dad are ordering pizzas for us, and there's lots of chips and pop. We set the basement up with a heap of mattresses. Dad's moving his big TV down there for us. It's always so much fun!" Georgia said to Mia. Georgia loved having all the girls over to her house for sleepovers. They could talk about boys, do their nails and hair, and stay up late watching scary movies.

The girls continued to plan their night until the bell sounded signaling the end of lunch.

"Mom! Mom?" Mia shouted.

"Yes, dear? What is it?" her mom answered from the kitchen.

"I got invited over to Georgia's house for a slumber party tonight. Is it okay if I go?" Mia asked her mom as soon as she walked in the door.

"Well, I don't see why not. Whose house is it at again?"

"Georgia's. Here's her mom's phone number. She's expecting you to call."

"Okay, I'll go call."

"I'm going to go and pack my bag and get ready." Mia said rushing off up the stairs towards her bedroom.

"Mia?" her mom called before she dialed.

"Yeah? What mom?" Mia called from the top of the stairs.

"Clean up your room before you go, honey."

"Okay, mom! Thanks, mom." Mia said walking into her room and pausing in the doorway to look around. Geez. Her room looked like a hurricane had gone through it. Mia sighed and started to pick her clothes up and throw them into the washing hamper. *This would teach her to let her room get so messy*, she thought with a sigh.

12

"COME IN, MIA! Oh, hi, Mia's mom, I'm Georgia. My mom and dad are in the living room, just through there," Georgia said, pointing vaguely toward another room as she took Mia by the hand and started dragging her away.

"Bye, mom! Thanks, mom!" Mia cried out as Georgia dragged her away.

"Where have you been, Mia? Everyone else is already here!" Georgia said as she and Mia walked into the basement where all the girls had gathered around in their pajamas.

"Mia!" Khloe cried out, hugging her as she walked in. "What gives? Where are your pajamas?"

"Party foul!" Sage and the other girls shouted. "Now you have to pay the price Mia Meatball."

Mia laughed. "You know I hate that name!

What's the price?" Mia asked as she pulled her pajamas out of her bag.

"Well. Let me think." Sage said screwing her face up in deep thought.

"She has to go first when we play truth or dare, so let's just go straight to dare!" Daylyn said from where she was sitting braiding Millie's hair.

"Too easy," Millie answered. "Pyjama run!" All the other girls clapped and cheered.

"Pyjama run! Pyjama run!"

Mia felt herself going bright red. She didn't need to ask what a pajama run was.

"Where and how far?" Mia asked slipping her pajamas on.

"Well, I think the usual run should be fine," Georgia said giggling. "What do you think Miss Captain?"

"Yep, sounds fair to me," Millie answered.

"Okay. So, you got to run down the street until you get to the convenience store and then back again," Georgia explained. *That didn't sound so bad*, Mia thought to herself. When her mom had dropped her off, they had passed the little shop, and it was only about a quarter of a mile down the road.

"But, there's a twist!" Khloe giggled. "You have to buy something from the convenience store!"

"No way!" Mia exclaimed louder than she had intended.

"Yes, way!" all the girls shouted back. *Damn it*, Mia thought to herself. This was going to be super embarrassing. All she'd brought was a long nightie, not expecting that she would be running down the street in the stupid thing.

"Okay, okay. I'm in. When do I have to do it?" Mia asked.

"Well, there's no time like the present. Let's go do it now!" Paige shouted. The rest of the girls agreed, so Mia started lacing her runners on. They all trooped upstairs past where Georgia's parents were chatting with Mia's mom and watching TV.

"Pajama run?" Georgia's dad asked, not even looking up from the TV.

"Yep!" Georgia shouted back as the group of girls flooded out onto the front porch.

"Be a dear, and go keep an eye on them," Georgia's mom said, patting her husband on the leg and pushing him up and off the couch. Georgia's dad sighed loudly, dragging himself up and off the couch.

"Okay, Mia. That's the store down there. Here's $5. Buy me a chocolate bar," Georgia's dad said chuckling as he handed her the money. "Don't worry. I'll be watching from here the whole time. The girls do this all the time," Georgia's dad said. All the girls had crowded out onto the porch and were waiting quietly for Mia to start running.

Here goes nothing, Mia thought as she took off down the street in her nightie.

"Go, Meatball!" Khloe shouted, cupping her hands together.

"You can do it, Mia Meatball!" Georgia screamed.

"Mia! Mia! Mia!"

"Run, Meatball, run!" All the girls were clapping, shouting, and cheering her on as Mia took off down the street. She burst into the convenience store loudly and startled the elderly store owner.

"Ai, you scared me, girl!" Mrs. Gonzales, the elderly store owner, said, putting her hand on her chest. "I swear, one of these days you kids doing your pajama run are going to give Mrs. Gonzales a heart attack!" Mia was out of breath from the run but quickly handed over the money while Mrs. Gonzales rang up the change on the cash register.

Just as Mia thought she was in the clear, she heard the jingle of the bells from the shop's front

door. Mia turned to look as two boys from her school walked into the shop. Both of them stopped dead in their tracks as they looked at Mia's nightie. Then, they burst into laughter. Mia could feel her face burning!

"Thanks!" She grabbed the chocolate and her change, then bolted for the door. The two boys followed her out and started cheering as Mia ran up the street towards her friends.

All the girls were out in the street cheering and shouting as Mia closed the distance to the house. They all grabbed her and patted her on the back, laughing as she jumped up the stairs and handed the chocolate bar over, her face still bright red.

"Thanks, Mia. Not a bad time either!" Georgia's dad said, laughing and taking the chocolate bar. "All right, you bunch of misfits and hooligans. Inside! No more pajama runs tonight."

All the girls were laughing and cheering as they headed back inside and downstairs to the basement.

"Great job, Mia. Because you were such a good sport with the pajama run, now it's your turn to choose something for the rest of us to do," Georgia said, throwing herself down onto one of the blow-up mattresses spread all around the basement.

"Hmm, umm, I don't know. What about truth or dare?"

"Oh, yeah! Now we're talking!" Georgia yelled excitedly. "Who are you going to choose first?"

"I choose...Khloe!" Mia shouted dramatically as she pointed over to where Khloe was eating chips. Khloe rolled her eyes. All the girls clapped and laughed, glad they hadn't been chosen to go first.

"Seriously? And here I thought we were going to be good friends. Anyway. Well, if it's up to me, then I choose DARE!" said Khloe in a loud, animated voice.

"Well, okay. I need to run upstairs and ask Georgia's parents if they have everything I'll need for your dare," Mia said, bouncing up off the mattress and taking the stairs two at a time, pausing halfway, "Georgia, come with me!"

"Oh great, you need to go and get stuff?! What are you doing to me? Oh, and just an FYI, I'm not shaving my eyebrows or anything like that if you're going to get a razor and shaving cream," Khloe warned. Georgia and Mia just laughed menacingly and whispered to each other as they closed the door at the top of the stairs.

A few minutes had passed, and all the girls were wondering what Georgia and Mia were up to when Georgia and Mia came running back down the stairs and into the basement with a backpack. All the girls giggled and whispered, shaking their heads and looking confused. Georgia didn't say anything; she just looked over at Mia and winked.

"Khloe, your dare, if you choose to accept it, is to wear whatever items of clothing are inside this bag, put on whatever makeup is inside the bag, then perform a dance routine for us to a song of my choice," Mia said with a dramatic flourish as she dropped the closed backpack next to Khloe.

All the girls burst into laughter. The basement was full of giggling girls all staring at Khloe, waiting to see if she would do it.

Khloe looked over to where Mia was sitting next to Georgia, slowly reached out her hand, and took the backpack.

"Game on, girls!" Khloe shouted as she headed into the washroom to get ready.

"What song did you choose?" Millie asked Mia and Georgia.

"You'll have to wait and see Mills!" Georgia

said, barely able to control her laughter as Mia burst into another fit of giggles beside her.

All the girls sat around talking to each other and trying to guess what Khloe would look like when she came out while they waited for her to finish getting dressed and doing her makeup.

"Okay, I'm ready! When I hear the music start, I'm coming out!" Khloe shouted from the washroom.

In the corner, Georgia plugged her iPod in and "Man! I Feel Like A Woman!" by Shania Twain came blaring out of the stereo. All the girls started laughing and clapping as Khloe walked out dressed in a black skirt, bright pink tank top, a blue mohawk wig, the brightest pink lipstick ever, and what appeared to be Georgia's big sister's wedge sandals.

Khloe was never afraid of being the center of attention and broke into what appeared to be a strange mix of ballet, hip-hop, and dabbing. The girls all stood up and started laughing and clapping, but most soon ended up rolling around laughing on the floor. As soon as the song finished, Khloe threw herself down onto her mattress, laughing and smiling.

"It's your turn now to choose someone for truth or dare, Khloe!" Georgia said.

"Lola," smiled Khloe.

"Truth!" Lola said without hesitation. Khloe then turned and asked Lola if she liked Ben.

All the girls are surprised Khloe would ask that since most of them had no idea Lola had a crush on Ben.

Lola blushed and whispered something so quietly none of the girls could hear.

"Pardon, Lola? You'll need to speak up. None of us could hear that!" Khloe shouted, getting into it now that it was her turn to embarrass someone else.

"Kind of! Yes! Is that okay?!" Lola said, her face now red as a tomato.

The girls all smiled and giggled.

"I knew there was something going on with all that art stuff! Okay, we won't harass you with questions right now, but if you guys like each other, then you need to tell each other."

The conversation continued for a while, with all the girls giving Lola dating advice. Then it was Lola's turn to choose someone, and the game continued. All the girls had their turn. They learned how hard it was to peel a banana with your feet and whistle with crackers in your mouth. The biggest news was that Lola was crushing on Ben.

After the game of truth or dare wound down, they spent the rest of the night talking about boys and hockey, hockey and boys: the girls' two favorite subjects. For Mia, it felt as if she had finally been accepted by the girls on her team.

As she drifted off to sleep, curled up on a mattress among the other girls on the floor in the basement, she was looking forward to seeing what the rest of the week brought and how the team would play in the upcoming tournament.

"So, how was the sleepover?" Millie's mom asked as she slipped into the passenger seat of her car.

"Not bad. No. It was great, actually." Millie beamed.

"Ah, see! I told you. So, you and the new girl, Mia, are getting along okay now?

"Yep. The rest of the team really like her too. It helps that she's such a strong player. I think we have a really good shot at taking the tournament next weekend."

"Well, I'm glad to see all you girls are getting along for once. Cameron's mom and dad asked if Cameron could stay over after practice on Tuesday."

"How come?" Millie asked. This would be the first time Cam had stayed over since he and Mia had become boyfriend and girlfriend.

"Oh, I think that Ryan is taking out Emma for their anniversary in the city. They're staying over rather than driving back so late." Millie was looking forward to having Cam stay over. It would give them a chance to hang out without all their other friends hanging around. Yep, a sleepover would be cool Millie thought.

13

"HOLY MACKEREL!" KHLOE gasped as she threw her goalie equipment down around her in the change room and collapsed onto the bench. "I mean, you all know I'm a goalie, right? I don't do the same drills as you. I'm special!"

"What's wrong Khloe? You look a little tired?" Georgia asked, laughing from the opposite bench.

"She looks like she's about to vomit!" Kiera, one of the juniors said with a giggle. Khloe frowned and took a long drink from her water bottle.

"No, well, maybe just a little," Khloe said as she laughed.

"Don't throw up in here! You'll make me throw up too," Mia chimed in. She finally felt relaxed enough around the other girls to join in with their banter. Tonight, out on the ice, the girls had trained well together. You couldn't even tell Mia was new.

"Ah, Mia Meatball, don't worry. Your meatballs are safe in your tummy," Khloe replied from beside Mia.

"Okay, everyone listen up!" Coach Phil shouted as he walked in. "Parents, can you wait outside for five minutes? I promise I'll be quick." The parents laughed and started to filter out. They knew Coach Phil meant what he said and wouldn't have them waiting around for ages like some coaches. As the door closed behind the last parent, Coach Phil sat down on the bench at the end of the change room and waited a moment for the chatter to stop.

"Right. Great practice tonight. Now, we have the first big tournament this weekend. Our draw looks good, but I want everyone focused on Friday. Get a good night's sleep on Thursday and take it easy Friday. I know I don't need to worry about all of you, but I like to say it regardless." The girls all laughed. It was the usual big-match speech by the coach, but all the girls liked to hear it anyway.

"Thanks, Coach!" the girls all chorused together.

"Who are we?" Coach Phil shouted.

"The Hurricanes!" the girls shouted back.

"What do we bring?" Coach Phil asked.

"The Storm!" the girls screamed back as they banged their sticks against the benches until the banging and racket sounded like thunder. Coach Phil held up his hands until the noise slowly started to subside to a low grumble.

"Thursday night's practice is a pass. Enjoy your night off and relax. If anyone needs a lift to the game on Friday, Saturday, or Sunday, just let me know, and I'll organize it for you. Have a great night, girls, and thanks for a great practice."

Millie watched the boys' team quietly, listening to her iPod, until the boys skated off the ice and headed into the change room. It didn't seem to matter how long she spent at arenas, watching practices. Ice and hockey were what mattered most to her, and while she watched the boys' practice, she liked to pretend she was plotting how to beat them and picking out weaknesses in their lines.

The boys' biggest fault was they all thought they were just so good, she thought with a laugh. They were good, but they weren't undefeatable. The girls had proven that already!

"Mills! I'll be out in two seconds. Can I shower at your place? Will your mom mind?" Cam asked as he walked past.

"Sure. Hurry up, though. I'm hungry. Mom's stopping for burgers on the way home," Millie answered, gathering up her iPod and headphones, slipping them into her hockey bag.

"Sweet!" Cam shouted back as he walked into the change room with the other boys. All the boys said hello or waved as they went past. Most of them had known Millie for as long as they had been playing, many of them starting off playing together in youth hockey teams when they were five.

Cameron came rushing out of the dressing room, still half in his hockey equipment. Millie stood up, and the two best friends walked towards the exit. As he got closer, Millie wrinkled her nose dramatically.

"You stink! Why do boys always stink so bad?" Millie asked.

"Ah, come on. You don't exactly smell like a bunch of roses either, Mills," Cameron shot straight back at her.

"Please. I'm surprised you even got a girlfriend you smell so bad!"

"I'm surprised I only have one! You keep it up, and you might get lucky with Rhys or Hunter. They like stinky girls!"

"Enough you two! I'm cold and hungry!" Millie's mom shouted from the car. "Ewww, Cameron you stink. You too, Millie. Hot showers as soon as we get home."

"See, even mom thinks you stink, Cam," Millie whispered, covering up a laugh with her hand.

"She said you stink too! You're not as pretty-smelling as you like to pretend," Cameron whispered back.

"You both stink! End of story. Now, we're almost at the burger place, so start thinking about what you want to eat."

"Bacon burger! Please," Cameron yelled out.

"Nuggets combo please, Mom!" Millie answered. Millie's mom just laughed. She didn't know why she had even bothered to ask. They ordered the same thing every time she took them.

"You two will be the death of me, and you, Millie, you might just turn into a chicken nugget one day!" Well, that set off both kids. They were laughing and giggling hysterically by the time they pulled into the drive-through. Cameron clucked like a chicken, which caused Millie's mom to laugh so hard that the lady working the drive-through speaker couldn't understand her.

As they drove home, quietly eating their food, Millie's mom thought to herself about just how lucky she was. She couldn't have asked for a better kid, and Millie couldn't have asked for a better best friend.

14

"OMG, the bantam boys' team is just so cute!" Georgia said, fanning her face dramatically like a damsel from an old western movie. The rest of the girls were busy checking the boys out for themselves, their faces pressed against the glass of the arena.

Millie laughed to herself. It was no coincidence that whenever the bantam boys were playing the girls, everyone seemed to show up five minutes early and get dressed and ready in record time.

"They're so dreamy," Daylyn and Ashlyn said in unison and sighed. The rest of the girls nodded and agreed.

"What are you all staring at?" Ben asked as he peered over the girls' shoulders, trying to see what they were all looking at.

"Umm, nothing," Lola stammered, blushing bright red.

"Oh, the bantam team. Seriously, what have they got that I don't? Sure, they're older, and they look like that guy out of Aquaman, and, oh never mind, I see why you're watching them now." This set all the girls off giggling again.

"When are you guys playing?" Ben asked.

"Not for another hour and a half. We gotta finish selling 50/50 tickets before the last game finishes. When are you guys playing?" Millie asked.

"We're playing in half an hour. The rest of the guys are getting ready, but I was here early scoring the last game, so I had a head start. How many tickets have you sold?"

"We sold the most!" Daylyn blurted out. Georgia groaned out loud.

"Yeah, it's hard to compete against twins that act adorable and say 'excuse me sir or maam, would you like to buy 50/50 tickets to help the youth hockey teams?' while four big hazel eyes look up at you. None of us ever stood a chance," Georgia said.

"On the flipside, they've sold so many tickets we almost sold them all in record time. Which has left more time to watch the bantam teams play!" Khloe said, giving Ben a big thumbs up.

"You're crazy. Anyway, I better get back inside for our team meeting. Don't forget to cheer for us. Bye Lola," Ben said quietly.

"Bye, Ben," Lola said blushing.

"Lola's got a boyfriend! Lola's got a boyfriend!" The girls all started cheering, making Lola's face go even more red, if that was even possible.

"Okay, enough. Let's go and sell the rest of the tickets so we can watch the boys play," Millie said, pushing Khloe and Georgia towards the arena doors.

The boys had a good game, but it was close. They came away with the win after both teams went into the last period with no score. Cameron scored the winning goal with only two minutes left on the clock. They managed to hold off the other team for the final two minutes to take the win heading into Saturday's games.

The boys were lucky enough to be running the gates, scoring, and operating the time clock for the girls' first game of the tournament. There was never any doubt the girls were going to win once the first period was finished. They were up three goals to zero and had already switched gears.

The tournament was based off wins and goals scored. This meant the girls wanted to post a good score and kept the goals coming through to the third period. They backed off halfway through the third to take the win 9-1.

"OMG! I can't believe I let that last goal through. It was almost an awesome shutout," Khloe moaned as the girls took their gear off in the change room.

"Don't sweat it, Khloe. You had an awesome game! We couldn't have done it without you," Mia said from the opposite bench.

"Yeah, Khloe, don't be so hard on yourself," Sage said, clapping Khloe on the back.

"What time is our first game tomorrow again, Coach?" Violet asked.

"Well, I have good news and bad news, Violet. Which do you want first?"

"Umm, bad news."

"We're playing at 7:00 a.m. The first game of the day."

"And the good news?" Millie piped up from where she was hanging the jerseys up.

"Ah, because we're the home team, our last game is at 7:00 p.m.," Coach Phil said with a laugh.

"Coach Phil! That's not good news!" Khloe groaned, trying to stuff her goalie gear into her bag.

"Yeah, it is Khloe. Just think about how much more time you'll have to sell 50/50 tickets and volunteer! Look, everybody, I know it's a long haul between games and hanging around all day, but I'm bringing in the grill and we'll barbeque at lunch. We're also going to have a team dinner at 4:00 p.m. for anyone who'd like to come. You guys had a great game today, and if we keep up this momentum, we'll be set for the rest of the tournament. Now, I want you all to get a good night's sleep tonight and be here at 6:00 a.m., ready for the game. All right, that's it from me. I'll see you all bright and early! And once again, great job. I'm proud of you guys."

The girls chatted among themselves while they finished getting ready. The early start and late finish sucked because it meant they'd be at the arena all day, but at least they had a break between games.

When Millie and Mia walked out of the change room, they noticed Cameron sitting on a bench by himself, waiting.

"Hey, Cam, I didn't know you waited behind," Millie said to him as they walked up.

"Hey, Mills. Hey, Mia. Yeah, I wanted to watch the two of you play, and my dad was going to be late anyway, so it worked out."

"Oh, thanks Cam," Mia said, blushing. It was still weird having a boyfriend that was actually interested in watching her play hockey.

"So, when is your dad coming?" Mia asked.

"I'm not sure. He got a late call to an accident, and mom is on night shift this week."

"Well, my mom is waiting outside. Why don't you crash at my house? And Mia, you could come over too. It would save your mom or dad getting up early. My mom will totally not care."

"That'd be cool with me. Can I get your mom to call my dad, Mills?" Cameron asked as they walked towards the carpark.

"I'll go and ask my mom if she can drop me off at your house after I get some PJs," Mia yelled as she headed over to her mom's SUV.

"She's great, Cam. You're lucky to have her as your girlfriend," Millie said as they walked over to her mom's car.

"I know, Mills, and I'm lucky to have you as a best friend."

"Aaaw. You'll make me blush. Hey, mom, is it okay if Mia and Cam stay over tonight? Cam's dad is working late, and we have to be here at 6:00 a.m. anyway."

"Sure, honey. Cam, I'll call your dad and let him know..."

"Mom said yes!" Mia shouted from the other side of the carpark. "I'll see you in fifteen minutes!" Mia shouted out the window of her mom's car as they pulled alongside.

"Are you sure you're okay with that Patty? I don't want Mia to be a hassle," Mia's mom said.

"Not at all! At least one of us will get her beauty rest!" Millie's mom shouted back.

"Thanks! My turn next time then. I'll run her home, get her showered, and drop her off."

"Sounds great. I'll order pizza, so don't worry about feeding her, and we'll have a glass of white while they get settled in."

"You're a champion. We'll be over shortly!" Mia's mom said as they pulled out of the carpark with Mia waving from the passenger seat.

"Never a boring evening with you two around!" Millie's mom said with a laugh. Cameron and Millie burst into laughter as they settled into the back seat.

15

DESPITE THE EARLY start to the next day, the girls came out on top of their opponents to take the win 6-3. The margin wasn't as high as the first game, but combined with the first game's score, it left the girls in a strong position before the last game on Saturday night. If they could get a clean sweep on their first three games, they would be able to skip the Sunday morning game with a by and head into the final on Sunday afternoon fresh.

The boys weren't having as much luck. Their first game on Saturday had been a hard match, with both sides never giving an inch. The opposition had scored two goals early in the first period, but the boys had only been able to answer with one goal late in the first period.

The opposition came out early in the second

period and scored again, but the boys couldn't find the net throughout the second period.

Going into the start of the third period, the boys were down 3-1 and couldn't seem to crack the defense of the other team no matter how hard they tried or what lines they switched up.

Georgia, Millie, Mia, and Khloe were now working gates for the boys' game and got to watch the entire game. It was heartbreaking seeing the boys try so hard and then lose, even if it was only the second game into the tournament.

They were waiting by the door watching as the boys lined up on the center ice to shake hands with the opposition after the game.

"Great game, guys!" Khloe shouted, cupping her hands together to make her shout echo around the arena. "Nice try, Logan! You'll get them next time."

"Thanks, Khloe." Logan fist pumped her as he went through the door. Khloe fist pumped him back; goalies had to stick together. Especially when one was having a bad day.

"Great game, guys. Better luck next time." Mia and Millie each said, holding out their hands for high fives as the guys left the arena dejectedly.

"You going to be hanging out after?" Cameron

asked, pausing to talk to Mia and Millie as the rest of the team filed into the change room.

"Cam! Change room. Now!" Coach John hollered.

"Yep, me and Mills are here all day to help out. Our last game's not for hours. Now, hurry up before Coach John loses his mind," Mia said.

"All right. See you guys soon!"

"I can't believe those guys beat us," Cameron grumbled for about the seventeenth time that morning.

"Cam, we got this. Stop stressing and focus on the next game," Preston said, patting Cameron on the back.

"Yeah. You're right. Thanks, Preston. So, what are we going to do for the rest of the day?"

"Want to have a game of ball hockey in the park?" Millie asked. "Boys versus girls, for old times sake?"

"Coach said we're supposed to be relaxing and saving our energy for tonight's game. He'd probably lose his mind if he saw us out there playing ball hockey."

"Yeah, I suppose. Or perhaps you're just scared of losing at ball hockey too!" Mia teased.

"As if! We aren't scared of losing to you. Just of Coach John. He would probably kill us. We have to help get the barbeque ready in a little bit if you want to help us with that instead?" Preston asked.

"Who wants a hot dog?" Preston's dad shouted from the grill. "Get them before they run off!" he said with a laugh.

Preston just groaned, while a few of the other moms and dads chuckled. His dad had a long list of dad jokes he liked to reel out at certain times or events. Always the same jokes, always at the same time.

"If we win tonight, does that mean we're going to get a by tomorrow morning Mills?" Khloe asked.

"Yeah. We'll be the only undefeated team if we win tonight because the team we're playing this afternoon is the only other undefeated team. So, we beat them and it's straight to the final game Sunday afternoon."

"Well, we better hope we win then because I need my beauty sleep," Khloe said.

"I think we all do," Georgia replied, "Except

me of course. I'm already perfect!" Georgia added, winking.

"Mia, I need you to work a bit harder in the corners. You too, Georgia. I know we've had a big weekend, but if we don't win this game, then we have to play again in the morning, and the Hellcats get the bye instead of us." Coach Phil said as Mia and Georgia came off the ice.

The girls had gone into the last game of the day full of confidence, but maybe they had been just a little bit overconfident. It was the last period, and they were down 2-1 with ten minutes left on the clock and no overtime.

"Next line, your up. Go!" Coach Phil shouted. "Switch, switch, switch!"

"They're weak on the left side, Mia. The left defense is weak. Go left and circle around right to score!" Millie shouted as she skated over and hit the door hard.

"Thanks!" Mia shouted as she hit the ice. Millie threw herself down on the bench, panting hard.

"Good pressure, Millie. I know you didn't score, but you outskated them hard. They're tired, and their recovery time is getting longer. Their coach has already shortened their line changes twice this period. The girls can't..." Coach Phil was interrupted as the buzzer sounded, and the arena erupted with cheers and whistles. Someone was even ringing a cow bell! Mia had scored, just the way Millie had told her.

"Okay, give Mia another thirty seconds, and then get ready to switch again, Millie. We've tied up the score, and I want to keep pushing them hard. Don't give them a chance to catch their breath."

"Okay, coach!" Millie said loudly, standing up ready to make the switch as soon as Mia hit the gate. Now that the scores were tied, it was going to be up to her and Mia to try and put another score on the board in the final few minutes of the game.

Mia skated hard into the gate, followed by the rest of her line, and fist bumped Millie as she jumped the boards and hit the ice.

"Get them, Mills!" Mia shouted.

Millie skated off just as the other team stripped the puck and started a drive up the ice. She swooped in from behind to try and steal the puck, but a misstep caused her to miss. *Calm down, Mills*, she thought to herself. *You have time on the board still, so settle down and relax before you mess it up.*

Ashlyn and Daylyn swooped in and stripped the puck from the opposition forward before they hit the blue line, completing what Millie had failed to do just moments before.

The opposition coach called a thirty-second timeout before the Hurricanes could take advantage, so Millie headed over to her own bench.

"Great pressure girls. Millie, Sage, Violet, you're going to split the middle, then go left. We already know that's their weak side. I don't need to tell you what to do; just do your thing, and I know you'll come through with the goods. Defense, be ready in case this doesn't pan out. We'll need to recover fast. Okay, get back out there and show them this is our town!"

Millie and the other girls hit the ice and did a quick fist bump before taking up their positions. The referee blew her whistle to signal the end of the timeout, and Millie started to move up the ice with Sage and Violet flanking her on either side.

Millie passed the puck to Sage as she skated alongside her. Then Sage and Violet passed the puck back and forth between them as they swung around behind the net. Millie moved to the right as the two wingers drew the defense in towards them behind the net. Just as the defense looked like it was going to overwhelm the two wingers, Maddie flicked the puck to where Millie was waiting close to the face-off circle.

Millie picked up the puck cleanly, and just as the goalie was trying to swivel back around to face the new threat, Millie sent the puck sailing straight into the net. The crowd went crazy as the other girls all piled onto Millie.

The girls skated past their bench and fist bumped their teammates on the way back to take up their positions.

The final minutes of the game were anticlimactic. Both teams were exhausted. The buzzer sounded, and the girls skated out onto the ice, and they all piled on top of Khloe. With their first three games won and done, the girls would get a well-earned rest heading into their final game on Sunday.

The boys had gotten ready early so they could watch the girls play just before their game started, so they went out on a high. The game itself was rather dull. The other team, having played and lost only a few hours earlier, came out onto the ice tired and rundown.

The boys started strong and scored three quick goals in the first period. They scored two more in the second period to head into the third and last period with a 5-0 lead. The other team came back hard in the third but only managed to put one score on the board while the boys added another.

The final score was 6-1, but it wasn't enough to guarantee a straight shot into the final game tomorrow, and the boys would need to play again in the morning.

16

THE GIRLS HAD turned up bright and early to support the boys in their semifinal match. Considering the tough course the boys had taken to get here, the semifinal match was pretty uneventful. That's not to say it wasn't a tough game, but the boys' win was never in doubt for a second.

Cameron scored twice early in the first period, and they cruised through the rest of the game, conserving their strength for the final. It was only late in the last period that the other team even tried to push the Lightning boys, but they had left it too late. The final score was 2-0 and meant that the boys would go through to the final later that day.

The girls had finished their volunteer duties on Saturday because one of the older teams took over on the Sunday, which left them free to focus on getting ready for their finals game.

"What time are you playing?" Cameron asked Millie as he walked out of the change room to where the girls and guys were gathered, talking and chatting.

"We're playing at 2:00 p.m. You?" Millie replied.

"Damn, same time on Rink 4," Cameron answered.

"Oh, that means we won't be able to watch each other play. That sucks," Mia said with frown.

"Yeah, I know, right? Anyway, we're playing the team that beat us Saturday morning again, so it's going to be a tough game anyway. You guys have a real shot though. No one has really pushed you yet. Do you know who you're playing?" Cameron asked the girls.

"Yep. That team we played on Saturday night. We were lucky they were tired. Apparently, they smashed the team they played this morning 7-1," Georgia chimed in.

"Seriously? Man, you better not let them shoot on me much tonight!" Khloe said sounding a little alarmed.

"Don't sweat it, Khloe. You can handle it!" Logan said, putting his arm around Khloe.

"Jeez, you two need to just kiss already, and get it over with!" Preston shouted from further down the bleachers. Khloe and Logan both blushed and quickly scooted away from each other while everyone else laughed.

"Leave them alone, Preston," Millie said laughing. "We already all know they're crushing on each other."

"Mills! Seriously, so much for friends!" Khloe shouted looking even more horrified, if that was even possible. Everyone laughed while Logan and Khloe just looked around mortified.

Both teams had a few hours to kill between games but were under strict instructions from their coaches to do nothing physical. The usual fall back for killing time in any tournament would be ball hockey, but the weather outside was horrible and both coaches were keeping a close eye on their players.

They decided on a massive game of Uno, with a boy and a girl from each of the teams pairing up together to play pairs. As with everything they ever did, the game degenerated into a farce, with more teasing, jokes, laughing, and giggles than actual card playing, but it did help pass the time.

The first period of the girl's final game set the tone for the rest of the game. The team they had previously beaten to make it undefeated to the finals were prepared for some serious payback.

They started the period off rough and showed the Hurricanes they weren't afraid to suffer the penalties. After the first period, the score was zero apiece, but the Hurricanes were getting pretty banged up.

"Girls, I know it feels like you're getting bashed around, but I need you to stay the course. Stick to the strategy, and we'll get through this. From now on, when they get a penalty, we need to capitalize on their mistake."

"But Coach..." Millie started to protest. It was one thing to turn the other cheek, but getting a battering in the process sucked.

"I know, Millie. I know," Coach Phil said, interrupting her. "It sucks, but instead of knocking them back, we need to ignore it and stay out of the box. Let the scoreboard do the talking for us, and after the game, we can gloat all the way home. Sound okay?"

"Yes, Coach Phil!" the girls all chorused back. It did suck, but winning and rubbing their opponents' faces in it afterwards would be oh, so sweet.

"Right then. Let's get back out there and play this game our way!"

The boys were having a rough game too, but not physically like the girls. The scoreboard was showing 2-0, and it wasn't in their favor. They knew they would have some serious competition this year, and so far, the tournament was a good indication of just how hard their season was going to be.

They went into the end of the first period with gloomy faces and without a score on the board.

They would need a seriously exceptional motivational speech from Coach John to pull them out of the funk they were in.

Midway through the second, Millie sat glaring through the glass of the penalty box as the rest of her team continued a player short. Coach Phil was glaring at her from the bench, and raised his hands up as if to say, *why*? She just shook her head and glared in a different direction.

"Stupid!" she shouted at herself. She was supposed to set the example, turn the other cheek, get a score on the board. Nope, not her. She got bumped once too many times and had bumped the girl back. Of course, the referee only saw her bump, and as a result, she found herself in the box for a two-minute body-check penalty.

Time always seemed to crawl by as you watched your team kill a penalty.

"You're out at the ten-minute mark," the time keeper said to Millie, pointing at the clock to make sure she understood. Millie nodded and stood up, ready to hit the ice and redeem her poor judgement.

Khloe stopped a shot on goal with her stick, and Ashlyn swooped in on the puck, sending it to the other end of the rink and getting an icing call, stopping the clock but allowing the girls to take the opportunity to switch lines.

"Ah, Millie, did we, or did we not, talk about our game plan?" Coach Phil asked quietly as she hit the bench.

"Yes, Coach," she replied, looking anywhere but at her coach's face.

"So, wouldn't it be fair to say that losing your temper and costing us a penalty is the opposite of our game plan?"

"Yes, coach."

"So, how about we stick to the plan from now on, Millie?!" Coach Phil shouted.

"Yes, Coach." Millie looked down at the bench, praying for the ground to open up and swallow her whole. The only bonus was that the other team hadn't scored because of her mistake, but the second period was almost over, and they hadn't scored either.

The boy's situation hadn't improved at all. It had actually gotten worse, and they were entering the third period 3-0.

"Look boys. I know this isn't what we hoped for, but you need to keep the pressure up. We've got a whole period left to play, and it's not over until the final buzzer. Okay?" Coach John was trying his best to keep the boys' spirits high, but there was a lot of hopeless expressions staring back at him.

"Coach John is right guys. It doesn't matter what the final score is. What matters is that we don't give up!" Cameron was up on the bench now yelling at the players. "So, what are we going to do?"

"Never give up!" the team screamed back at Cameron just as the buzzer sounded to signal the start of the third period.

"That's right guys! Now get back out there and bring the thunder!"

The third period was almost over, and neither of the girls' teams had managed to put a score on the board. With less than four minutes left, Coach Phil was trying every play he could think of to get that puck into the net.

No one wanted to head into overtime, or worse, a shootout.

With less than one minute on the clock, Coach Phil called Khloe out of the net and threw Mia out onto the ice. With his two best players on the ice, he was sure they would break through the other team's defense.

"Left and right?" Millie asked Mia as they skated down the ice. Mia didn't reply, she just nodded and kicked up the speed a notch until they were both flying down the ice.

As soon as they hit the blue line, the two girls

split apart, one going left and one going right, drawing the defenders out of the middle. Their goalie's head looked like it was on a swivel, swinging from left to right as the two girls got closer and closer.

At the last minute, Millie flicked the puck across to Mia, and Mia slapped the puck towards the goalie's head. The puck went flying high and flat, and the entire Hurricanes bench was on their feet, but at the last moment, it hit the cross bar and dropped down onto the ice at the goalie's skates.

No goal! The buzzer sounded a second later, signalling the end of the third period and the start of overtime. The girls on the ice skated back towards the bench, the disappointment clearly etched on their faces.

"Okay, it was worth a shot. Great try, Mia and Millie. Sudden-death overtime is set for two five-minute periods, with the first team to score taking the win." No one liked sudden-death overtime, but if no one scored in the next two periods, then it would go to a shootout, and that was even worse. "Stick with the game plan, and let's grind them down!" Coach Phil shouted.

The boys had lost their final 3-1, with Preston scoring a miracle goal in the last few minutes. Despite the loss, their spirits were still high as they came off the ice. They didn't head into the change room, instead detouring over to where the girls were just starting their second sudden-death overtime.

"Damn, they are going hard out there. Everyone looks exhausted," Preston said to Cameron as they stood against the glass of the arena.

"What happens if no one scores during the last sudden death?" Logan asked, looking up at the clock above the scoreboard.

"They have twenty seconds left in this overtime period, and then it goes to a shootout," Cameron answered just as the buzzer sounded. "Just like this."

"OMG! I hate watching shootouts. I never know which way to look," Sage groaned from the bench. The rest of the team was on their feet, cheering as Georgia took the ice.

It was now up to the three best shooters from each team to shoot on the net to determine the winner. In a shootout, one shooter from each team shoots on the goal simultaneously. Each team gets three shots, and the team with the most goals after all three shots wins.

They all knew it wasn't the best way to settle a game, but when you've already gone to double overtime and the game is still deadlocked, there aren't many options left.

Georgia skated towards the opposing goalie, going hard and straight. She wasn't messing around. At the last minute, she faked left and put the puck straight into the top right corner of the net. Unfortunately, the other team pulled a similar move on Khloe and scored as well.

"You're next, Mills. Don't miss!" Georgia said as she skated into the bench.

Great, thought Millie, *just what I need: more pressure.* Millie skated out to center ice and waited for the referee to signal that it was time to go. The girl from the other team looked just as nervous as Millie felt.

"I think I'm going to throw up," Mia said watching from the bench.

"You'll be fine. It's just another shot on net. No pressure." Coach Phil said, patting her on the back. Mia just groaned. She hated shootouts.

Millie looked down the ice at the goalie, and the referee blew her whistle, signaling that it was time to go. She kicked off hard but then slowed a bit, trying to take a quick look at the goalie. She had watched Georgia and knew that if she copied her, the goalie would be waiting and ready for the fake, so she decided to double bluff.

"She's going to double bluff," Georgia said from the benches. "She's skating my exact line."

"What's that mean?" Kiera, one of the juniors, asked.

"Well, she'll make it look like she's going to do exactly what I did. Except when she fakes left, she won't shoot right. She'll shoot left. The goalie will expect her to shoot to the right just like I did," Georgia explained.

As Millie skated towards the net, she followed Georgia's skate marks and could see the goalie's eyes tracking her. Just as she got close to the crease, she faked left and watched the goalie flinch and then start to move right. A quick flick of her wrist sent the puck low and to the left. The goalie didn't have enough time to recover from her move to the right, and the puck shot into the net.

As she skated around the net, Millie looked to where Khloe was and saw her shake her head. Damn it. The other team had scored again too.

Now it was all up to Mia.

Mia skated out onto the ice and waited for the referee's signal while the rest of the team lined up on the bench nervously waiting. She could hear her parents cheering her on but shut out the noise and focussed on what she had to do next.

The referee blew her whistle, and Mia started off, skating hard and fast. She was going straight for the five hole. Hard and fast straight down the center.

"She's going for the five hole."

"How do you know, Mills?" Georgia asked from beside her.

"She doesn't have a lot of options left. It's either that or she repeats what either you or I did."

Mia didn't miss a step as she flew down the ice. The goalie was shimmying left and right in her crease, trying to anticipate which way Mia would go.

Mia faked to the right, saw her chance, then put her shot straight through the five hole.

The entire arena erupted! Khloe had gone low at the other end and stopped the other girl's goal! The Hurricanes had won! All the girls and coaches flooded the ice, heading towards Mia and Khloe. The boys watching around the arena were cheering and banging their sticks on the glass. The arena was going crazy!

After they finished their pileup on the ice, the girls all lined up to shake hands with the other team before lining up again to receive their medals. The head of the local skating organization presented each of the girls with a medal, and Mia received a trophy for player of the tournament. Millie was presented a trophy for team of the tournament because of their winning percentage. All the girls posed for photos out on the ice before they headed for the change room.

"Great game, Mills! Awesome shot, Mia!" Cameron shouted as the other boys formed an honor guard for the girls to walk through on their way to the change room.

"Thanks, Cam!" Millie said as she led her players off the ice.

"Thanks, Cam," Mia replied, giving her boyfriend a big hug.

Cameron hugged Mia back and turned bright red, much to the delight of the other boys, who all teased him.

The girls had won the tournament final after a thriller game, taking the entire tournament in a clean sweep. The boys hadn't been so lucky, but it

was only the first tournament of the year, and the season had a long way to go.

Mia was finally a part of her new team and had quickly become friends with Millie and the other girls on the hockey team.

What will the rest of the season have in store for the boys and girls of the Lightning and Hurricanes?

The End

HOCKEY
WARS 3
THE TOURNAMENT

TURN THE PAGE FOR A SNEAK PEAK

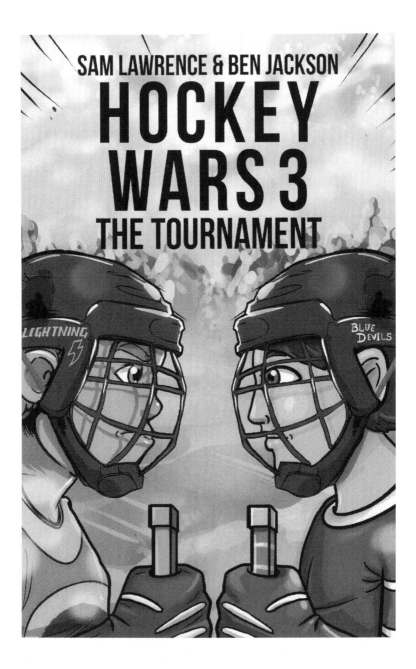

1

"ALL RIGHT, EVERYONE! A bit of quiet!" Coach John shouted across the bus. Coach John had been coaching the boys' hockey team, the Dakota Lightning, for several years now but knew most of the boys and girls from both teams. "I know you're excited for our first away tournament of the season, but I have to get the rules out of the way. Who knows the rules and wants to help me out? Cam? Millie?"

1. No messing around on the bus and throwing stuff while we're driving.

2. No messing about in the hotel after the coach calls lights out.

3. Between games, it's time to relax and rest for the next game, but at the end of the day, it's time for fun.

4. Most importantly, represent the Dakota Hurricanes

SAM LAWRENCE & BEN JACKSON

and Dakota Lightning like your family, but have fun and don't forget where you come from!

Cameron and Millie took turns shouting out the rules. They knew them all by heart, but some of the other younger kids hadn't been away on tournaments, so it was all new for them. Millie was the girls' captain and Cameron was the boys' captain. They used to play together when they were younger, but as they got older, they split into boys' and girls' teams.

Initially, this had led to a lot of drama, especially as they were best friends. It had all come to a head the year before, but a grudge match had sorted it all out, and now they were closer than they had ever been.

"Thanks, you two! That's right. Play hard, but remember, we're all representing our teams." Coach John looked them all in the eye. "Hey, don't worry. Coach Phil is giving your parents a lecture about behaving and having fun on the other bus right about now too."

All the kids laughed and giggled, imagining their parents being told to behave themselves.

"All right, enjoy the rest of the trip. We have about another three or four hours until we arrive at the hotel." The kids all clapped and cheered, and Coach John took a bow before settling into his seat and talking to some of the other adults that had ridden on the kids' bus with them.

"So, how's it going with you and Cam?" Violet asked Mia, leaning over the leather seat to try and talk to Mia two rows back. Violet played forward for the Hurricanes and was dating Linkin from the boys' team.

"Shh, he's just over there!" Mia said, shushing her friend as she blushed. Mia had joined the team at the start of the season and was currently dating Cameron, the captain of the boys' team.

"Please, half the bus heard that. For sure Cam did!" Linkin shot back at Mia, laughing hysterically. Linkin was usually one of the quieter members of the team, which was funny because he played defense for the Lightning, and his large size usually made people assume he'd be big and loud. He'd been coming out of his shell lately, however, and his signature black pants and red plaid shirt was never far away from any action.

"Enough Link! Mia's already embarrassed enough without you making it worse. Sorry, Mia. Sometimes I don't realize how loud I'm talking. Forget the boys. Are we going to take home this trophy this year? I don't want a repeat of last year!"

"I'll second that!" Millie said. Last year at the same tournament, the Staten Saints had come out of nowhere to smash the Hurricanes in the final. They'd been up five goals up, with only ten minutes left in the last period, when the Saints had not only leveled the scores but had gotten one up with only seconds left on the clock.

"I still can't believe that happened," Khloe said angrily. Even though it wasn't all her fault, as the goalie, she took a lot of the blame on her shoulders. Even the best goalie could only do so much without the support of her teammates, but that game had turned her from hero to zero in ten minutes flat, and it still stung.

"Shake it off, Khloe, that's not happening this year. We're going to be right beside you. Nothing is getting through," Millie said as she leaned over and hugged Khloe. No one blamed Khloe, but they all knew every goal that slid into the net was a personal defeat for the bubbly, quirky goalie.

"Has anyone stayed at this hotel before?" Logan asked loudly from the back seat, his question silencing the chatter on the bus almost instantly. Logan was the goalie for the Lightning and seemed to be continuing the strange tradition of goalies being just a little bit odd. Logan was also

Millie's cousin, which made him very protective of the Hurricane's captain. On and off the ice.

"Logan? Let's keep it down, buddy," Coach John said from the front of the bus, rubbing his forehead dramatically, not even bothering to turn and identify the loud culprit. You could guarantee if someone was loud, it was Logan. *It was going to be a long bus ride*, Coach John thought to himself.

"Sorry, coach!" Logan shouted back, barely stifling a laugh.

"Seriously dude, you're going to get us in trouble," Rhys muttered under his breath, "and that's my job!"

"You're just jealous someone's getting more attention than you, Rhys," Mia added, jumping to Logan's defense. Even though Mia had joined the girl's team at the start of the season, she had fit right in, soon becoming close friends with all the girls and boys from both teams.

"You think we can clean sweep the away tournaments this year?" Cam asked the group of boys sitting around him.

"Taking Icefest would be a start. I've heard they have some of the best swag," Ben chimed in. Ben was one of their biggest and strongest defensive players, but he had an artistic side too. He loved to draw comics and had created some impressive hockey-related comics based on the two teams. He also had a massive crush on Lola, the Lightning's left wing.

Lola, too, loved to hang out with Ben and draw and was secretly crushing on him back, but so far, they had both been too shy to make the first move.

"What sort of swag?" Linkin asked.

"Well, I heard the winners all get the usual medals and a trophy, but they also give away a sweet Bauer equipment bag filled with stuff."

"That would be awesome!" Cam said joining in.

The rest of the long bus trip was relatively uneventful, with most of the kids talking and gossiping. A round of singing competitions had been quickly stopped by Coach John, who had announced the contestants on American Idol had nothing to fear from this group of kids and that he couldn't listen to their "screeching" another minute longer.

As the bus pulled up in front of the large hotel, the kids all scrambled to look out the windows.

"Look at the sign!" Mia shouted excitedly, pointing towards the front of the hotel.

WELCOME ICEFEST PLAYERS! GOOD LUCK!

"All right. Before you all run off, we need to check in. Now, it's already late, so no pool tonight. Just hang out in reception until all your parents are checked in, then head up to your rooms. We have a big day tomorrow, so plenty of rest—no mini sticks in the hallways, and no running around the place. I'll see you all bright and early for breakfast at 8 a.m. Have a good night's sleep!" Coach John finished speaking and stepped aside, barely avoiding being knocked over as all the kids rushed off the bus.

It was going to be a big day tomorrow, and the kids were full of energy now, but by this time tomorrow night, they'd be completely drained. It was a long weekend, and Coach John hoped they would be able to come away with the win by the end of the tournament.

NOTE FROM THE AUTHORS

As Indie authors, we work hard to produce high-quality work for the enjoyment of all of our readers. If you can spare one minute just to leave a short review of our book, we would greatly appreciate it!

Let everyone know just how much you and your children enjoyed *Hockey Wars*!

We are currently working on expanding this series so stay tuned for future updates by following us on Facebook or visit our website!

www.facebook.com/benandsamauthors

&

www.benandsamauthors.com

Thank you, Ben and Sam ☺

Made in the USA
Columbia, SC
03 December 2019